THE HEART OF A KING

The Tudor Saga Series
Book Six

David Field

SAPERE
BOOKS

THE HEART OF A KING

Published by Sapere Books.

20 Windermere Drive, Leeds, England, LS17 7UZ,
United Kingdom

saperebooks.com

ISBN: 978-1-913335-69-4

I

A pleasant aroma of burning pine logs wafted from the blazing fire in the side chamber inside Hatfield House as Elizabeth Tudor sat silently contemplating the momentous news she had been brought. An hour earlier, the Lord Chancellor of England, Nicholas Heath, had ridden to Hatfield, the chosen residence of Elizabeth, to surrender to her the Great Seal of England and to advise her that following the death of her sister Mary she was now Queen of England.

Since the arrival of that first group, which had included Elizabeth's Surveyor of Estates and trusted adviser, William Cecil, and her lifelong friend, Robert Dudley, many more had dismounted at the front door, as an impressive number of the nation's nobility, including many of the previous Council of State, lost no time in offering to swear their loyalty to their twenty-five-year-old Queen.

Elizabeth turned to the man on her left with pleading eyes. 'What must I do, Cecil?' she asked.

'Think you that you have a choice, my Lady?' Cecil replied. 'The day has finally arrived and you are Queen of England. That must be the last time I address you in the old way, Your Majesty.'

'Address me as you see fit, Cecil,' Elizabeth replied, 'since it is your counsel I would have, not my correct style and title.'

Cecil nodded towards the dividing doors behind them. 'You must soon show your face out there and give those assembled their first indication of how the nation is to be governed in the future.'

'But what should I say?'

'Whatever it pleases you to say, since the nation will henceforth be governed by your will and inclination.'

Elizabeth gave a slight tut of irritation and turned to the handsome man of her own age seated on her right, placing an urgent hand on his tunic sleeve. 'Dearest Robert, give me the words.'

'The last Dudley who sought to place words in the mouth of a Queen lost his head on Tower Hill, Your Majesty. I do not wish to follow my father down that same path.'

'Fie, both of you!' Blanche Parry, the fourth member of the intimate group, protested. 'You have long since assured my Lady that you act always in her interests. Now, when she has most need of your counsel, you fall silent.'

Cecil smiled at this rebuke from Blanche and transferred his benevolent gaze to Elizabeth. 'I will not presume to give you the words, Majesty, but I will suggest the theme.'

'Anything, Cecil,' Elizabeth pleaded. 'There are those enough already who think me a frivolous girl. How would it be were I to make my first address as Queen in anything less than sensible words, designed to convey my fitness to rule the realm?'

Cecil appeared to think for a moment, then gave his first advice to his new monarch. 'Few will be persuaded to leave this place until advised of who is to be appointed to what. We may begin with your Privy Council. It must be smaller than it had become under your sister, when every man and his fool seemed to have a say in the nation's affairs.'

'How many, say you?' Elizabeth asked.

'We cannot be prescriptive of numbers. I would hope to be deemed worthy of a seat in my own right and clearly you must include those senior officers of State such as the Lord Chancellor and the Earl Marshall. Likewise, those consecrated into the sees of Canterbury and York have traditionally been honoured with a place at the table, although if you would accept my well-meaning advice you will limit the number of prelates, at least until the detailed future of our nation's religion has been agreed. As for the remainder, they must be an astute combination of those you trust and those of whom you are suspicious.'

A look of alarm crossed Elizabeth's face. 'I must clasp vipers to my bosom?'

'At least while they are at your bosom, you know where they are,' Cecil replied with a knowing smile. 'Would you rather have them around your Council table, where they bear collective responsibility for such policies as are agreed, or out in the wilderness, where they may plot and scheme unseen?'

Elizabeth nodded at the wisdom of that, then turned to Robert Dudley. 'If I may have men about me that I trust, why not Robert, my newly appointed Master of Horse?'

'Should you wish, Majesty, although it may prove necessary to elevate him into some other office, in order to justify his seat in Council.'

'It shall be done, Cecil, but what of yourself? I once asked you — almost in jest — if you would be my Chief Minister. I am now asking you, as your Queen, to whom you owe every action, every thought and every loyalty — will you head my Council?'

'I will and with humility, Your Majesty, if only to protect you from those who might be inclined to give you ill advice designed to unsteady your grip on your throne.'

'Ah yes, my enemies,' Elizabeth sighed. 'Who do you propose?'

'Fortunately,' Cecil replied, 'the worst of them are no longer available, since Norfolk and Gardiner have been consigned to the flames of Hell. But there is still the Earl of Pembroke, along with his uncle, the Marquess of Northampton. They served as Gentlemen of the Chamber to Philip of Spain, who has not taken kindly to the recent changes. They say Philip skulks in the Low Countries, awaiting the appropriate moment to invade.'

'He once proposed marriage to me,' Elizabeth reminded him.

'And he is likely to repeat that proposal, Your Majesty,' Cecil replied, 'which is one of those matters that we must consider before we summon your first Council. But before that, there is the all-important matter of the nation's religious observances. You have often expressed to me your desire that all men should be free to worship as they wish, but unfortunately something stronger will be needed to reassure those of your Reformist subjects who have been subjected to such indignities these past five years that they did not suffer in vain.'

'I must declare England a Protestant State, say you?' Elizabeth asked nervously.

Cecil shook his head. 'Not in so many words, but you must be seen to promote the new forms of worship while ordering no reprisals against Catholics. It will not be an easy path to tread, but I will guide you.'

'What else should be on the table for my first Council meeting, and when shall it be?'

'We must lose no time,' Cecil told her, 'and so tomorrow suggests itself, here at Hatfield. And in answer to your first question, you must give clear guidance on your preferred foreign policy.'

Elizabeth grimaced. 'Given that I shall provide Philip of Spain with the same answer that I gave to his first proposal of marriage, should he have the effrontery to burden me with another, we should be seeking an alliance with France, should we not?'

Cecil sighed. 'Would that we could, Your Majesty, but therein lies another difficulty. As you will be aware, the young Queen Mary of Scotland is now married to the Dauphin of France and will one day rule as its Queen also. My spies at the French Court advise me that some months previously she made a secret will in which her crown of Scotland and her claim to the English throne were both bequeathed to France, should she die without issue. An alliance with France would be unlikely to persuade anyone over there to foreswear that legacy and our only hope of preservation, were we to face simultaneous invasion from both France and Scotland, would be an alliance with Spain. And, of course, Mary Stuart is Catholic by conviction.'

'So, apart from the matters of religion and foreign policy, there remains the issue of my possible marriage?' Elizabeth asked, somewhat testily. 'And the latter two are closely allied, are they not? England's future relations with the other nations of Europe will depend upon who shares my marriage bed.'

'Regrettably, it was ever thus,' Cecil replied quietly, with as much sympathy and tact as he could summon. 'One of the burdens of royalty is that they may never marry where their heart lies, but must choose a bed partner in the best interests of the nation.'

'No doubt you have someone in mind already, Cecil?' Elizabeth asked frostily. 'And am I to even be consulted in the matter?'

'Of course, dearest Lady,' Cecil assured her. 'My men are even now touring the Low Countries for someone suitable, and should one emerge, you will of course be consulted before any negotiations commence.'

Elizabeth made a disgusted noise, then looked back defiantly. 'And why the Low Countries, pray tell me?'

'First and foremost, because of the importance of our trade links with the cloth houses of Flanders. Secondly, because they have persevered with religious reform even in the face of their occupation by Philip of Spain and we must be seen to give them every support, if we are to maintain the loyalty of those of your subjects who follow the Protestant faith.'

'But thereby further antagonising Philip of Spain?' Robert Dudley interjected.

Cecil nodded. 'Regrettable, but perhaps the lesser evil of the two.'

Elizabeth had been thinking deeply and now pierced Cecil with a defiant stare. 'What if I should let it be known that I do not wish for marriage — to anyone?'

Cecil looked momentarily horrified. 'What then of the succession, Your Majesty? If there are no heirs, then Mary Stuart will have not just a strong claim to England, but the only claim. England will be in thrall to both Scotland and France and will be plunged back under the rule of Rome.'

'So I must dedicate my womb to England, is that the best advice you can offer me?' Elizabeth demanded with obvious distaste.

Cecil nodded and looked down at the table, unable to meet her ongoing defiant glare. At that moment the servers appeared through the rear door that led down to the kitchen via the service stairs, intent on clearing the board, and Blanche Parry rose to her feet.

'Forgive me, my Lady, but I must see to the matter of dinner.'

'Dearest Blanche, did you imagine that your fortunes would not rise with mine?'

'My Lady?'

'Now that I am Queen, I shall require Ladies, shall I not? Would you consent to be my Senior Lady?'

'With all my heart, Your Majesty — but what of Mistress Ashley? She was in your service before me and has ever served you loyally and devotedly.'

Elizabeth gave a light laugh as she reached out and kissed Blanche's hand. 'Think you that I do not reward such devotion? But Kat has a husband who heads my household estates and would be burdened by his absence were I to keep her constantly by my side, as I hope to keep you. I shall appoint her "First Lady of the Bedchamber", while finding some accompanying position at Court for Sir John. This means that I shall still require a Senior Lady, who will also be my closest personal confidante and friend. Do you shrink from such responsibility?'

'Of course not. I shall be delighted,' Blanche managed, before the tears rolled freely down her face and she rushed from the room.

Cecil also rose and to mask his discomfort in the face of such open emotion sought leave to withdraw from the chamber in order to make the necessary announcement regarding the composition of the new Council of State. This left Elizabeth alone with Robert, whose face had grown solemn.

'Why so glum, dearest Robert?' Elizabeth asked.

He hesitated for a moment before replying, 'In truth, it is all this talk of your marriage. My heart breaks to think that you shall be required to share a bed with a man for whom you may have no feelings.'

'That will never happen, Robert, let me assure you,' Elizabeth insisted. 'Perhaps for that reason, I shall never marry.'

'Has no-one claimed your heart?' Robert asked.

Elizabeth replied to the mullioned side window, 'There is one, but he is married to another.'

'And if he were not married?' Robert persisted.

Elizabeth blushed and dropped her gaze to the floor. 'Have you no duties in the stables? Does my Master of Horse neglect his position on only the second day?'

As Robert bowed and took his leave, Elizabeth watched his departure. Then as the heavy doors close behind him, she whispered, 'If only I were not Queen and you were not spoken for. But England now has first claim on my affections.'

II

It was time for the progress to Westminster Palace for Elizabeth's coronation. The procession passed slowly uphill and Elizabeth watched the tableau that Robert had conceived. It was a mock castle gateway emblazoned symbolically with red and white roses in equal numbers, from whose battlements Court musicians perched perilously as they performed specially commissioned fanfares. Above the gates hung a series of portraits, also commissioned specially for the occasion. On the lowest level were the Tudor grandparents, Henry of Richmond and Elizabeth of York, and above them were Henry and Anne Boleyn, who in turn gave vertical birth to Elizabeth herself. The whole was well done and Elizabeth hoped within herself that the imagery was not lost on those who gazed at it — the blood coursing through her veins came direct from the victory at Bosworth.

All the way to Cheapside the narrow jettied buildings had disappeared under a forest of banners, heraldic devices and streamers, while on their doorsteps stood the solemn city merchants adorned in their liveries and hoods. The progress was halted while the Mayor presented her with a gift from the city, in the form of a purse of crimson satin filled with a thousand gold marks.

Elizabeth rose to her feet inside her chariot. 'I thank my Lord Mayor, his brethren and you all. Be ye ensured that I will be as good unto you as ever queen was unto her people. And persuade yourselves that for the safety and quietness of you all, I will not spare, if need be to spend my blood. God thank you all.'

This drew thunderous applause, to the diminishing sound of which the progress carried on through Ludgate, before the city took its farewell at Temple Bar and the cavalcade came to a halt at Whitehall Palace, where Elizabeth stepped down from the carriage and walked sedately into her private quarters accompanied by Blanche Parry.

'When do we transfer to Westminster Hall?' Elizabeth demanded of Robert Dudley, who had been waiting anxiously in the Withdrawing Chamber.

'Not until the morrow,' he replied, 'but what thought you of the pageantry?'

'It was meet enough,' Elizabeth replied dismissively, 'although it must have been very costly.'

'Your subjects wished no expense spared in their demonstration of their love for you,' Robert explained by way of justification.

'Their love of pageantry, you mean — not to mention their happy excuse to get roaring drunk and pick each others' pockets.'

Robert looked helplessly across at Blanche Parry, who indicated with a slight jerk of the head that he should withdraw to the Audience Chamber before the royal temper revealed itself more fully. Once the opportunity presented itself, Blanche slipped outside to join him and placed a consoling hand on his sleeve.

'You must not be discomforted, Robert. My mistress has a headache brought on by all the clamour and din of the progress. Added to which, she was nervous as to how her subjects would receive her.'

'Why nervous? Does she not know that all England is at her feet?'

'You must make allowances, Robert, given the years in which she feared to lose her head at the whim of her sister. She needs reassurance that she is loved, but she is too proud to admit it. When she is suitably composed, I will come back out and lead you back into the presence.'

'Do I now require a summons before I may attend upon the lady with whom I was wont to ride through the grounds of Hatfield?'

'Have patience, Robert,' Blanche urged him. 'She has much to readjust to.'

'As, it would seem, do I,' Robert replied peevishly as Blanche slipped from his side and re-entered the Withdrawing Chamber.

As the Audience Chamber filled to capacity, Robert sensed someone at his elbow as he continued to gaze down at the courtyard, where even now the royal grooms were taking the bridles of tired mounts as their noble riders dismounted. He turned, and Cecil smiled reassuringly.

'Well done, Robert. Our mutual friend presented a fine queenly image, thanks to your tireless and gifted efforts.'

'Yet she is still a girl,' Robert sighed. 'A frightened girl, what is more,' he added as he nodded towards the closed doors leading to the Withdrawing Chamber. 'She skulks in there with a headache and in one of those petulant moods that she has displayed since childhood, and which now betray her womanly weakness.'

'I have served her these many years also, in my capacity as her Surveyor of Estates,' Cecil reminded him, 'and I know her capacity for loyalty to those who display loyalty to her. She requires but a short period in which to adjust the crown of England on her head and she will become the old Elizabeth once more, you will see.'

As they had been speaking, the heavy doors had been opened wide and out walked Elizabeth, followed a few feet behind by Blanche Parry. There was a heavy rustling sound as brightly hosed knees descended to the carpet and Elizabeth gestured daintily with both hands that everyone should rise. Then she addressed them in a clear voice that gave every indication that she had embraced her new role.

'I thank you all for your attendance, both here and in the progress from the Tower. Be in no doubt that such love and loyalty as you have displayed will not go unrewarded. I shall formally become your Queen on the morrow, but even today I am able to assure you that the future of England is in the forefront of my heart and mind. You should now all disperse to your homes, that we may all be refreshed for tomorrow's momentous event.'

With that she bowed and turned to walk back into her Withdrawing Chamber. Blanche Parry hesitated for a moment, caught Robert's eye, then nodded. He walked towards the heavy doors, one of which was unceremoniously opened for him by the page who had its management.

On the other side of the door, Elizabeth did her best to repair the damage. 'Please forgive me, dearest Robert, if I was somewhat churlish when first I came in from that wondrous progress that was all of your making. As Blanche will have advised you, I took one of my sick headaches from the clamour and stress of it all. I owe you much gratitude.'

'I did it all out of love of you, Lillibet,' Robert assured her as he took her hand and kissed it. 'Not the love that is due to a monarch by a loyal subject, but the love of a man for a woman.'

'Please Robert, no more in that vein!' Elizabeth begged him. 'Say rather the love of one lifelong friend to another. And so what of tomorrow's ceremony and the vexatious matter of the raising of the host?'

'It is all agreed to your satisfaction,' Robert assured her. 'At a moment during the Mass shortly before the host is to be raised, the Bishop will indicate with a gesture of his head and you may move behind the rood screen to St Edward's Chapel that will mask the raising from your sight.'

'What of the banquet to follow?' Elizabeth asked.

'All in hand and the finest seen these many years, although no doubt you will rail against the cost.'

'You will take the seat beside me at the banquet?'

Robert looked back lovingly into her eyes. 'Nothing would keep me from your side on such an occasion. But it will be a long evening, I fear.'

'And you must ensure that I do not over-indulge in the wine, Robert, since I must meet with Cecil the following day in order to agree the agenda for the first official meeting of my Council two days thereafter.'

'At least I may rest at home during those days, since I am barred from your Council.'

Elizabeth pouted. 'Let us not renew that argument, Robert. It would not be good for the image of my rule were it worded abroad that my Council is padded with favourites.'

'I am but one favourite,' Robert countered, 'although hopefully the greatest of these. Why would you not wish the counsel of those who love you most dearly?'

'For that very reason,' Elizabeth replied testily. 'As Cecil advises me, I must ensure that the counsel I receive is not what I wish to hear, but what I *need* to hear. Those who love me most dearly would be inclined to give me my head, which might not be best for England. If it is of any consolation, you will of course join me for dinner after the meeting of Council and I will advise you of what transpired.'

'I shall be at home, as I previously mentioned.'

'But it is a short journey from The Strand,' Elizabeth reminded him.

'I was referring to my house at Throcking.'

Elizabeth's eyes widened in a mixture of apprehension and disbelief. 'You go back to reside with your wife, when you are required here by my side? I forbid it!'

It was Robert's turn to stare blankly back at her. 'You would deny a man access to his own wife, after all he has done in your service these past weeks?'

'This particular man, yes,' Elizabeth insisted. 'You are to attend me at all times, in your capacity as Master of Horse, until such time as I no longer require you at my side.' Their eyes locked in mutual defiance and the ominous silence was only broken when Elizabeth tossed back her dark red locks and told him, 'That is a command, Robert. From your Queen.'

Sunday 15th January 1559 was an occasion to remember with awe. The winding procession along the freshly laid blue carpet was so long that its vanguard had reached the wide open doors of Westminster Abbey before the tail had left Westminster Palace. First to hove into view were the carriers of the four massive Swords of State, the Earls of Derby, Rutland, Worcester and Westmorland. They were followed by the Lord High Steward, the Earl of Arundel, bearing the sceptre and slightly behind him, carrying the orb of State, the Lord Treasurer and Marquess of Winchester. A few paces behind came the crown, proudly held aloft by the Earl Marshall of England.

Then the ecstatic crowd pressing against the barriers caught sight of their new monarch, decked out in the traditional finery. As Elizabeth stepped up to the prepared throne in the centre of the crossing the ceremonials began and over an hour later the new Queen emerged back into the frosty sunlight, holding the orb and sceptre with all the tenderness appropriate for newborn infants.

She was now 'Elizabeth, by the Grace of God, Queen of England and Ireland' and God preserve anyone who dared argue otherwise.

III

'Remember, when we go in there, that above all your Council are praying for a resolution of England's religious practices.'

Elizabeth nodded silently at Cecil's sage advice, then reached out to take Robert Dudley's hand. 'Would that you could be by my side in there,' she murmured.

'Good luck, my Lady,' Blanche Parry said as Elizabeth rose and nodded for Cecil to precede her into the Council room at Whitehall Palace.

The assembled members rose in unison and the nervous murmuring of conversation died instantly. Sir Nicholas Bacon, in only his second day as 'Lord Keeper of the Great Seal' took a deep breath and spoke with as much confidence as he could muster. 'I speak for all the members of this humble Council when I offer my heartfelt congratulations on Your Majesty's coronation and assure you that our every loyal thought and effort shall be towards the prosperity of the realm that you now grace.'

Elizabeth indicated with a delicate hand gesture that the Council members should resume their seats. 'I thank all of you for those good wishes, gentlemen,' she assured them, 'and hope that you are content for the business of this Council to be managed by my most trusted adviser William Cecil, who will henceforth be known as the Secretary of State for England.'

The defiant look that accompanied the announcement left no-one round the table in any doubt that any objection would have serious career consequences and the only response came in the form of nods and whispered expressions of agreement.

Elizabeth nodded down the table for Cecil to open the proceedings.

'At this most propitious of times,' he began, 'there are several matters which it is beholden of us to consider as a matter of some urgency. The first is the future of the nation's religious observances.'

'More burnings?' came the anxious enquiry from Matthew Parker, former Dean of Lincoln, seated halfway down the table.

'And why not?' demanded William Barlow, soon to be Bishop of Chichester and an ardent Reformer who had spent some years in exile to avoid the wrath of the late Queen Mary. 'If it was good enough for true believers such as ourselves, why not the damned heretics who blaspheme daily by raising the host?'

Elizabeth raised one hand and it fell anxiously silent. 'It is precisely that outpouring of bitterness and revenge that I wish to avoid. No, my lords, there will be no burnings, but neither will Catholic abominations be allowed in our churches. We are met to find some compromise between the two. The Church established by my illustrious father shall no longer be sullied by heathen practices and superstitions such as have previously disgraced our divine worship. We shall re-issue the English Book of Common Prayer that was the proud legacy of my late brother Edward and we shall insist that all men attend the simple service conducted each Sunday in each parish, or be fined.'

'And how does Your Majesty intend to punish the heathen Catholics?' was Parker's next question.

Elizabeth smiled graciously and replied, 'I shall not punish them for what lies in their hearts, unless it be treasonous.'

It fell silent and Cecil came to her rescue. 'What Her Majesty means is that she has no wish to punish by law what may be the true urgings of men of any religion, of whatever form. She will, however, come down most heavily on anyone who allows the passion of their religious beliefs to curdle into rebellion against her throne.'

'You will tolerate any form of worship?' Barlow said incredulously.

'What men feel in their hearts — even practice in the privacy of their homes — shall be a matter of conscience between themselves and God,' Elizabeth replied serenely. 'We shall only proscribe what they do in our churches.'

'And Your Majesty will do so as the Supreme Head of the Church of England?' Parker asked.

Elizabeth shook her head. 'I shall govern the Church, certainly, but I will not set myself up as its supreme head in the manner that you suggest. For one thing it would proclaim me as some form of prelate and for another it would not do for a woman — even this woman — to preside over a religious hierarchy.'

'And yet you must be seen to be at the apex of our Church in some way,' Parker argued, 'in order that our religious observances may be seen to be one and the same as our national identity.'

'Perhaps "Supreme Governor"?' Cecil suggested gently from the far end of the table and when Elizabeth looked down at him with raised eyebrows he nodded gently in a sign that she should consent. She thought silently for a moment, then nodded.

'If it will move this debate forward, then so be it.'

A sigh of relief went round the table as this most difficult of issues was safely circumnavigated, although they must now descend to points of detail.

Back inside the Withdrawing Chamber Robert Dudley was showing signs of boredom and impatience. He'd got up and stared out of the window several times, had sat for some minutes drumming his fingers on the side table from which Elizabeth's needlework had been tactfully removed by Blanche Parry and was now peevishly prodding the fireguard with the toe of his boot under the anxious gaze of the 'Queen's Senior Lady', who was seated in a corner with her own needlepoint.

'Have patience, my lord,' she urged him quietly, 'since they have much to discuss.'

'And I have much business of my own to conduct,' Robert reminded her petulantly. 'Does she intend to keep me penned in here daily, like some sort of hunting mount in a stables, only to be taken out when there are deer to be pursued?'

'You are important to her, as am I,' Blanche assured him, 'and she will wish our reassuring company when she comes back.'

'If I am that important to her,' Robert retorted with a pointed nod at the dividing door through which the low drone of conversation was audible, 'why am I in here and not in there?'

Blanche put down her needlepoint. 'In there, my Lady is Queen of England. In here she is Elizabeth Tudor and can relax among those who love her most honestly, without thought of personal gain or preferment.'

'It was Cecil who talked her out of my having a seat on her Council, was it not?' Robert demanded. 'He fears that she loves me more and will therefore be more inclined to listen to my counsel.'

Blanche thought hard before replying, then steeled herself for what had to be said.

'You speak of my cousin and the man who steered my Lady safely through those terrible years in which her wicked sister sought her downfall — perhaps even her death. In addition to that, he has the ear of every noble in England and has some thirty years of skilful negotiation and Statecraft behind him. Is it better that England be guided by Cecil, or that Elizabeth be counselled by you?'

As they sat at supper, Blanche looked discreetly away as Elizabeth held Robert's hand. Cecil was absent on business of his own and Elizabeth was hoping to enjoy a pleasant evening in her most favoured company before she was obliged to face her Council again the following day.

'So what does Cecil require that you turn your mind to on the morrow?' Robert asked.

Elizabeth tutted. 'Why must you spoil these most pleasant of times with thoughts of Council business, my sweet?'

'Because — *my sweet*,' Robert replied with heavy sarcasm, 'It is the only way I may know how you will be spending the morrow, since I will, I assume, be required to return here to share your breakfast. I have two questions. The first is where your mind — which of course means Cecil's mind — is directed regarding an alliance. Surely it must be with France?'

'Why "surely"?'

'Because an alliance with Spain would encourage that dreadful Philip to seek again for your hand in marriage. You have already declined him, and in my hearing.'

'I was not free to marry at that time, since my sister was still alive and he was married to her.'

'But he will renew his odious entreaty, will he not?' Robert persisted. 'If — as you seek to assure me — you want none of him, then surely our best alliance lies with France?'

Elizabeth inclined her head from side to side in a gesture of uncertainty. 'That was my first thought also, but Cecil advises that France means us no kindness. The Catholic Mary is set to rule France as consort to the Dauphin, while her mother Mary of Guise resides back in Scotland, where she daily gathers more and more French troops to her side. We are surrounded on both sides should they continue in their Catholic opposition.'

'Is there no remaining Protestant presence in Scotland?' Robert asked. 'And if it is simply a matter of driving French troops from Scotland, why may I not lead your army north?'

Elizabeth leaned sideways. 'The very nation that only a moment ago you were suggesting that we seek an alliance with? It is as well that I have Cecil to advise me. But you said you had two questions. What was the second?'

'Linked with the first,' Robert said warmly as he leaned in towards her and kissed her lightly on the lips, ignoring another cough from Blanche Parry. 'If you are to refuse Philip of Spain because your heart lies elsewhere, who is that lucky man?'

'Ask me again when you are no longer married, Robert,' Elizabeth replied under lowered eyelids. 'And now, if you have supped adequately and we are to avoid scandal, you must reclaim your horse from the stables.'

The 'private business' of Cecil's was an invitation to the London lodgings of the Spanish Ambassador Gomez de Feria, who — or so rumour had it — was shortly to be pensioned off by his lifelong friend and patron Philip of Spain. Cecil had little doubt of the reason for the invitation and de Feria got straight to the point as he handed Cecil a goblet of sherry and waved him into the seat by the fireplace.

'Now that you are Secretary of State, my dear friend, you will be able to persuade your Queen that it is in the best interests of England to accept the ongoing offer of marriage from my master King Philip.'

'There are two serious assumptions built into that question, my Lord Ambassador,' Cecil replied. 'The first is that Her Majesty would be open to any persuasion on my part and the second is that a marriage with Spain would be in England's best interests.'

'You realise that you are surrounded by the French? Over your northern borders in Edinburgh, as well as across the Channel?'

'I would be a poor Secretary of State if I did not keep myself daily acquainted with the location and disposition of the nation's potential enemies. By such means, for example, I am aware that your master continues to hold down the Dutch and that our friends and trading allies in the Low Countries are little better than slaves under his dominance. As a Protestant nation, England must not be seen to ally with Catholic oppressors.'

'Is that why your envoys are seeking a husband for Elizabeth in the Low Countries?'

Cecil smiled condescendingly. 'You are to be congratulated on the efficiency of your spies, Ambassador, but they have presumably also advised you that as yet no suitable prospect has been identified.'

'And if such a man were identified, would Elizabeth do your bidding?'

'She is my Queen, Count de Feria, not my horse,' Cecil replied starchily.

The Ambassador inclined his head in a gesture of apology. 'A thousand pardons, my lord, but my real question was whether or not the rumours are true and that the only man with access to Elizabeth's heart is her Master of Horse.'

'It is true that they are close,' Cecil replied evasively, 'but you forget that Dudley already has a wife.'

'A sick wife, or so I hear,' de Feria replied. 'A malady of the breast, I am informed. What then, should she die?'

'We will meet that eventuality when it arises,' Cecil replied sharply. 'For the moment you may advise your master that should he wish to formalise a proposal of marriage, it will be treated with the honour that it merits.'

IV

Both Elizabeth and Cecil soon came to realise that they had been lulled into a false sense of security by the ease with which the religious reforms had been steered through Council. This was obvious on the second day allocated for discussion of pressing matters, when the clamour of differing opinions around the table regarding which nation England should seek an alliance with suggested that this would be far from easy to agree upon.

As could have been predicted, the traditionalists — and most notably those of a Catholic persuasion — were in favour of an immediate and enduring peace treaty with Spain, preferably reinforced by a royal marriage. Their arguments barely rose above the obvious one that Philip of Spain was currently the most powerful monarch in Europe and by virtue of his stranglehold on the Low Countries was well placed to wreak havoc on England's cloth trade. Cecil was obliged to remind those in favour of such an alliance that the matter of a possible royal marriage was down the agenda for discussion on a later date when they began clamouring vociferously for Elizabeth to lose no time in letting the Spanish Ambassador know that she would look favourably upon a proposal for her hand from the man whose navy also dominated the trade routes to the New World.

Cecil seemed to be talking to himself until those with Flemish sympathies, and most notably those who represented the city merchant guilds, reminded their pro-Spanish opponents that an alliance with the most powerful nation at any given moment in history could prove unwise if those fortunes were reversed. Then Cecil was obliged to reverse his arguments and remind those assembled that the only other major power in Europe was France, which had forever been allied with Scotland in 'the Auld Alliance', whose common enemy was England.

'Does anyone around this table seriously argue that France would agree to be allied with us under the present conditions?' Cecil challenged, but there were no responses.

'This means, does it not, that it must therefore be Spain?' argued Earl Marshall of England Thomas Howard, Fourth Duke of Norfolk, a man as committed to 'the old order of nobility' as his grandfather had been. He was one of those whom Cecil had counselled Elizabeth to keep close by her side in order to prevent him plotting in dark corners, as had his grandfather of the same name before him. Thomas Howard had been raised as a Protestant, largely for reasons of advancement, but his family tree was heavy with the fruits of Catholicism and his loyalties were suspect.

'It by no means requires that we ally with Spain,' Cecil replied, bracing for the obvious response, which came back across the table at him without mercy.

'You have just ceased reminding us why it would be unwise to ally with France and yet now you insist that it cannot be with Spain either?' Thomas Howard demanded. 'Is there any nation on God's earth that you believe fit to receive the blessing of your approval?'

There were a few suppressed titters and Elizabeth was so angered to see her loyal friend being baited like a chained bear by this upstart young stripling that she could not refrain from interrupting. 'When you have the years of experience with which my loyal Secretary of State is blessed, my Lord of Norfolk, then you may perhaps acquire the ability to appreciate subtlety of argument. The Secretary merely brings to our attention the dangers implicit in selecting either France or Spain as an ally.'

'But each of their Ambassadors is eagerly awaiting a decision,' Howard countered.

'Then let them wait,' Elizabeth glared back at him. 'When the day arrives that my nation is at the dictate of foreign ambassadors, then you may criticise the Secretary for his sage advice. You fail to appreciate that closely tied with the issue of an alliance is the matter of who shall share the royal bed. Unless you are about to propose that England's foreign policy be decided on the basis of which of the various contenders for my virginity I most lust after, then be silent and listen to the advice of your elders — and wisers.'

'Thank you, Your Majesty,' Cecil replied as Howard went bright red in the face. 'In the circumstances,' Cecil continued, 'given that I have fully explained the options, it might be best if we now adjourned for dinner, returning in two hours time to bring more considered counsel to bear on the matter.'

Once inside the Withdrawing Chamber Elizabeth grabbed Cecil's arm with a pained expression. 'Did I overstretch my authority in there, dearest Cecil?'

'On the contrary, you put that young coxcomb in his rightful place,' Cecil said. 'And given that you are Queen, what limit do you think exists to your authority?'

'But we are no closer to choosing an alliance partner,' Elizabeth reminded him.

'Nor shall we be if we sit there for a week. That was my whole object, since our decision, if we ever reach one, will bear heavily on your choice of a husband, as you yourself reminded us.'

Elizabeth's face soured as she walked to the table on which dinner was in the process of being laid and poured herself a goblet of wine. 'Let us not forget that there is more to this than either my hand in marriage or an alliance. There is the matter of a royal heir and whichever nation its sire shall come from will have a claim to the English throne. Should it be Spain, then Philip achieves the ambition with which he married my sister and England becomes merely another gem in the Habsburg crown, and what then of our Protestant friends in the Low Countries? If France, then my heir will be related in some manner to the Catholic Mary when she becomes Queen of that nation and we may expect her Scottish troops across our borders, along with those Frenchmen who currently lurk in Edinburgh, no doubt waiting to strike. Little wonder that I hesitate.'

'We can delay any decision in Council for some time yet,' Cecil told her as he also helped himself to wine. 'This will allow us more freedom of choice and will also no doubt lead to other offers for your hand.'

'From where, exactly?' Robert Dudley said, as he rose from his seat and came to the table, reaching out for Elizabeth's hand. 'This English rose is far too delicate a plant to be exposed to the rough wind of either France or Spain. And why do we need an alliance with any other nation, say you, if it will mean that our dear Elizabeth is forced into a marriage she would no doubt detest?'

'You consider that England is strong enough to survive without any alliance?' Cecil asked with raised eyebrows.

Robert nodded. 'I say that it could be. While Philip of Spain was escaping from his marriage bed with Mary, he spent many days in our new dockyard at Portsmouth and he took me with him. He is well aware of the current weakness of our navy, while he continues to add to his. Our only possible threat comes from across the Channel, whether it come from France or Spain, and it would be my counsel that we increase our navy to such a degree that it rivals that of Philip. Then we may tell him where he may put his proposal of marriage.'

'And the cost of such a venture?' Elizabeth queried.

'A new shipping tax, which would happily be paid by those of our merchants who rely on our strong presence in the Channel,' Robert replied. 'Once we have a navy worthy of the name, we may also strike west, to those lands from which Spain currently draws its wealth in gold, spices and sugar. We may also send men and ships in search of even greater wealth elsewhere.'

Cecil snorted. 'You know of a man who could bring all this about?'

'I know of at least two,' Robert defied him. 'Whilst in Portsmouth I made the acquaintance of a Devon man named John Hawkins, who was highly regarded by Philip for his services in transporting ambassadors from the port of Cadiz. His family are ship owners and builders down the road in Plymouth and he is anxious to expand his fleet so as to open more trade with the Indies. He is skilled in the science of navigation and ambitious for personal fortune. If we encourage the expansion of his fleet, perhaps with a little money from the privy purse, then such vessels as he builds would do service as armed merchantmen should we be threatened with invasion. And of course we can replenish the money that comes from the Exchequer by way of monopoly grants for his trading.'

'And the second man that you mentioned?' Cecil asked.

'He exists here at Court,' Robert replied with a smug smile. 'He is Her Majesty's astrologer, Dr Dee.'

'An astrologer who builds ships?' Cecil enquired sarcastically.

'An astrologer who is also a mathematician and much taken with the science of navigation by the stars and the use of mathematical devices to chart the progress of ships across the oceans. His science, and Hawkins's ships, could open up new trade routes that would put the Spaniards to shame, thereby swelling the Treasury in time of peace and converting newly built vessels into warships should we be challenged by either Spain or France.'

Cecil's eyes had been glowing attentively and now he turned to Elizabeth. 'There would seem to be some merit in what Robert suggests, Your Majesty. Perhaps he should be commissioned to journey to Plymouth and seek out this man Hawkins?'

'No!' Elizabeth protested, to everyone's visible surprise. 'I need Robert here by my side at all times. Better that Master Hawkins be summoned to London. And now perhaps we should eat.'

Cecil and Elizabeth took a seat each and began carving into the roasts with their dining knives. Robert continued to stand by the table, watching them and swilling wine contemplatively around in his goblet.

Elizabeth looked up anxiously. 'You do not join us, Robert?'

'In truth I have no appetite, after all this talk of your marriage to a foreign prince.'

'Well, you can strike one from the list,' Elizabeth announced as she turned to Cecil. 'Have the Spanish Ambassador advised that I have declined Philip's odious offer of marriage, although I have no doubt that you will frame it in more diplomatic language. Now then, Robert, will you sit by me at this board and eat something?'

After Cecil had excused himself, Robert turned once more to Elizabeth.

'It is tedious sitting here, day after day, while you accompany Cecil to meetings of your Council, from which I am banned for reasons that I still fail to understand,' he muttered.

'Your constant presence here is of great comfort to me, Robert, as you well know,' Elizabeth replied. 'It gives me relief from the tedium of Councillors and their self-serving prattle. By the same measure, were you to attend me in Council you would become, to me, just another dreary aspect of my duties to my people and there would be no relief when I come back in here. Many a day have I sat listening to my Councillors arguing among themselves and comforted myself that before long I may return to your loving company.'

'Only to be dismissed once it is time to retire for the night and I must risk life and limb in the darkened streets, on horseback, with only one sturdy manservant to deter footpads.'

'Footpads, even here in the centre of London?'

'Particularly here in the centre of London,' Robert told her. 'They grow more numerous by the day, as the city grows richer and the pickings therefore more tempting.'

'Would you be easier in your mind were you to have chambers here at Whitehall?'

'Only if they were also yours,' Robert whispered as he reached out and stroked her cheek.

Elizabeth pushed his hand away gently and made a chiding noise with her throat before replying. 'I shall choose to ignore that, since encompassing a violation of your Queen would no doubt constitute treason.'

'Only if it were not welcomed,' Robert reminded her as he reached across to touch her breast. Elizabeth pushed him away and Robert's face darkened. 'I shall require to be absent from here for some nights in the near future anyway,' he continued, 'since my wife is due to visit me at my town house.'

'You must not lie with her!' Elizabeth blurted out instinctively, then reddened deeply from the neck upwards.

'She is my wife!' Robert protested. 'Do you presume, as Queen, to deny a man the pleasure of lying with his own wife?'

'They say she is sick,' Elizabeth replied with the first excuse she could muster, 'and surely it does not ease any sickness to engage in carnal activity?'

'That rather depends upon the nature of the sickness, does it not?' Robert replied archly. 'But should it be your royal command that I refrain from lying with my lawfully wedded spouse, then of course I must obey. Now, if you would excuse me from the royal presence, I must resume my nightly evasion of footpads.'

He rose from the table, bowed to a sarcastically low level and strode out through the door that led to the Audience Chamber.

Later, as Elizabeth and Blanche sat opposite each other before the fire, each engaged upon their needlepoint, Elizabeth had a question. 'Blanche, are there any vacant chambers on this floor?'

'Indeed there are, my Lady. Two chambers from your bedchamber is another that was once used by Kat Ashley and her husband on days when they were engaged here at Whitehall. Since Kat is now required here barely once a week, she and Sir John have removed themselves back to Hatfield and when here they make use of one of the suites left available for visiting dignitaries on the floor below. Why do you ask?'

'I wish Robert Dudley to be accommodated here, rather than his having to risk his life in the darkened streets when he leaves us late each evening. Who is the person in my service who can make that empty chamber a bedchamber for Robert?'

'Your Chamberlain, Lord Howard.'

'My great uncle? Excellent!'

'You wish me so to instruct him, my lady?'

'Perhaps, but first remind me. This chamber lies two away from mine, you say?'

'Yes, my Lady.'

'And between these two chambers?'

'A spare chamber that we are holding in readiness for when there should be any royal children.'

'And these two chambers — mine and the one that might be designated for Robert — are kept locked from either side of this middle chamber?'

'Yes, my Lady.'

'The keys thereto being held by my Chamberlain?'

'Yes, my Lady.'

'You understand my drift, Blanche? There must be no suggestion that Robert and I had access to each other through this middle chamber.'

'Indeed not, my Lady. Do you wish me to instruct the Chamberlain to make the necessary arrangements?'

'No, Blanche. Have him attend me before breakfast on the morrow, ahead of the arrival of Robert Dudley for another day of cooling his heels in here.'

Within days, the lascivious rumours were raging like wildfire through the Palace of Whitehall regarding the new accommodation for Robert Dudley. From there the tittle-tattle spread throughout the wider Court and into the city and hardly a person could be found in London who was not salivating at the mental picture of the beautiful Queen going to it with the handsome Courtier with the shapely calves. Council knew of it by the end of the first day and Cecil was steeling himself to raise the matter with Elizabeth when the admission of the Spanish Ambassador into his chambers was announced.

'Are the rumours true, William?' de Feria demanded.

'What rumours would they be, my Lord Ambassador?' Cecil replied with a serene countenance that masked a darker apprehension.

'That your Queen has finally chosen to give her body to her Master of Horse — do not play the pretence game with me, Master Secretary.'

'I am of course familiar with the same rumour that has come to your ears,' Cecil replied with a hint of annoyance, 'but since I am not retained to advise Her Majesty on where her body should lie — simply what her policies should be — I can neither confirm nor deny that rumour.'

'She dishonours my master Philip of Spain!' de Feria all but shrieked.

'How so?' was Cecil's reply.

'He has offered her his hand in marriage and she disports herself with a horse groom!'

'You must forgive me if, due to pressure of business of late in the Privy Council, I completely neglected to advise you that Her Majesty thanks your master for his courtesy, but graciously declines his offer of marriage.'

'She prefers to fuck with a stable groom?' de Feria demanded, red of countenance.

'Again, I am not privy to that information, my Lord Ambassador. I am instructed only to advise you that she will not be fucking with Philip of Spain.'

'My master shall hear of this!' de Feria thundered.

Cecil smiled back insultingly. 'Indeed, is that not the function of an ambassador?' he asked. Then he chuckled briefly as de Feria stormed out, swearing copiously in his native tongue, before the reality sank in. It would soon be the talk of Europe and Cecil was praying to God that it was not true.

V

Cecil was bustling down the side corridor from his office chambers in Whitehall when Thomas Howard stepped out into his path with a smirk.

'On your way to do Her Majesty's bidding, my lord? Or in a hurry for an early dinner?'

'Step aside, Norfolk,' Cecil instructed him, 'since I am indeed engaged in the Queen's business and she will not be best pleased if I am delayed in conducting it.'

'Only a few weeks ago the entire Council would be summoned in order to advise Her Majesty,' Howard sneered by way of reply, 'but it seems that she likes not our counsel of late. Or is it more the case that she is over-tired through lack of sleep?'

'Your meaning?' Cecil demanded curtly.

Howard allowed the leer to remain on his lips. 'Well, while she might enjoy a good night's sleep in her own chamber, I am advised that she gets little of it in the chamber where she lies each night.'

'One should not listen to rumour,' Cecil told him defiantly.

'Indeed, I do not,' Howard replied reassuringly, 'but you forget that her Chamberlain is a Howard.'

'Good day to you, my Lord of Norfolk,' Cecil glowered as he dodged around him and strode off muttering under his breath. He had received enough bad news for one morning. King Henry of France had been killed in a tourney and the sixteen-year-old Mary of Scotland was now Queen Consort of France to his successor Francis II, a somewhat weakly fifteen-year-old who was entirely dominated by his wife's staunchly Catholic uncles from the House of Guise, Duke Francis of Guise and Charles, Cardinal of Lorraine. Their sister Mary of Guise, Mary's mother, was championing the rising Catholic cause back in Scotland, where she was acting as Regent until her daughter by James V came of age. It was the Guise influence that had led to so many French soldiers assembling in Edinburgh and its immediate suburbs and by their very presence seeking to intimidate the Protestant faction into silence.

As if this were not bad enough news, the Protestant resistance movement had lost control of Edinburgh to Mary of Guise and were now seeking England's support for a resurgence campaign. Morally and tactically England was bound to respond favourably and it was a perfect opportunity to smash the 'Auld Alliance' once and for all, leaving a friendly, grateful and Protestant neighbour north of England's border at Berwick. But the English Treasury was all but bankrupt and had none left of the old warriors who had led previous Tudor armies in their forays against both the French and the Spanish.

It was therefore with some trepidation that Cecil sought audience with Elizabeth and found himself, instead, alone with his cousin Blanche Parry.

'Where is your mistress?' he asked.

Blanche gestured towards the dividing doorway. 'In there, dressing for the day's business, beginning with your morning audience.'

'Will she be long, think you?'

'Long enough. She takes great care with her many layers of garments.'

'Dear cousin,' Cecil said softly, 'sit here with me for a short while, for I have something of great matter to discuss with you.'

They took a seat on the banquette under the window and Cecil placed an urgent hand on Blanche's sleeve.

'You have heard the rumours, of course?'

Blanche dropped her gaze and blushed. 'Regarding my Lady and Robert Dudley?'

'Are there any other rumours?' Cecil grimaced. 'In truth, I hear nothing else, from my Steward to my stable groom, all agog with the prospect that I know more than I am telling. So what do you know that you are not telling, cousin?'

Blanche continued to blush, but remained silent and Cecil came at the issue from another direction.

'The chamber that lies between Elizabeth's and Robert's — it is empty, is it not?' When Blanche reluctantly nodded, Cecil pursued his line of questioning. 'Why do you not occupy it? It was surely intended that someone such as the Queen's Senior Lady would be accommodated in there, that she might be in attendance on her mistress at any hour of day or night?'

This prompted a reluctant nod from Blanche. 'This was the original intent, no doubt, but in truth I have never occupied that chamber, since as you know I have my own suite of rooms on the floor below. It is being held empty in prospect of royal children, should there be any.'

'It is kept locked on both sides?' Again Blanche nodded, but her expression became more furtive as she anticipated the next question. 'And the keys thereto?'

'With the Chamberlain, but...' She bit her lip and lowered her head even further.

'But what, Blanche?' Cecil demanded sternly. 'We both serve Elizabeth, but we would both best serve her by your revealing the truth.'

Blanche's voice dropped to a whisper. 'It may not be truth, but rumour has it that my Lady has a spare set, on a string that she wears around her neck and close to her skin under her chemise, that none may see it.'

'None but those who are in there as we speak, dressing her?'

'Yes. She ordered new servants of the wardrobe some weeks ago and when I questioned why I was being excluded from those duties she claimed that it was to preserve my dignity as her Senior Lady.'

'Dear God!' Cecil muttered, just as there was movement from the inner doorway and Elizabeth appeared, dressed as if for a day among her Courtiers. She held her hand out for Cecil to kiss like any other Courtier, then took her usual seat at the table set for breakfast, while Blanche scuttled away with her head down, after muttering that she would order food from the kitchen.

'Is this breakfast or dinner, Your Majesty?' Cecil asked pointedly.

Elizabeth shot a defiant look back at him. 'I obviously over-slept, but is that such a sin?'

'That rather depends upon what led to it, does it not?' Cecil replied guardedly, 'and you will forgive me for my presumption, but there are ugly rumours in circulation regarding why you might require to sleep late. On the subject of which, where is Robert?'

'I will forgive your impertinence, given our long friendship, Cecil, but am I to assume that you have also succumbed to those rumours?'

'I had hoped to obtain Robert's guidance, as a soldier, as to what we must do to assist our friends in Scotland.'

'I was not aware that we had any and Robert has not been in battle since his last hopeless foray into the Low Countries at the side of Philip of Spain. You surely do not expect me to commission him back onto his warhorse?'

'Perhaps not, but it were best discussed when he is present. When do you expect him?'

'By the hour. He has merely ridden to organise his house in Kew, ahead of an anticipated visit by his wife. The second this year.'

'You resent her?' Cecil asked suspiciously.

Elizabeth shook her head. 'I am not one of those who you may undo with sideways questions, Cecil. At least while Robert has a wife, those ugly rumours to which you refer cannot grow into wild suggestions that we are about to wed. Although that would relieve me of one of the more tedious unresolved matters of which you are no doubt here to remind me. If so, this will be a brief conversation. But given that the food is arriving in front of us, please join me.'

It was some minutes, and several helpings of cheese and manchet loaf, later that Elizabeth recalled their earlier conversation.

'You have news from Scotland?'

'Indeed, Your Majesty, and of the gravest. As you will know, Queen Mary now holds both it and France in her Catholic grip and our Protestant friends in Scotland are seeking our aid in driving out the French troops brought in by the Regent Mary of Guise. They have recruited to their cause the former Scottish Regent James Hamilton, the Earl of Arran, who is distantly related to Mary but resents that the Scottish crown belongs to her and not himself. He is also a Protestant and has written to me offering a permanent peace and a final end to the so-called "Auld Alliance" with France if we will send English troops to enable him to retake Edinburgh, overthrow the Guise faction and rid Scotland forever of French men-at-arms.'

Elizabeth's face lit up. 'This is good, is it not?' she asked.

'It would be, Your Majesty, had we the money with which to equip an army.'

The page announced Robert Dudley's entry and he threw himself into a vacant chair and reached across the table for the wine jug.

'Cecil here is just advising me that we have no money to raise an army,' Elizabeth told him.

'Are we being invaded?'

Cecil shook his head. 'We are being invited to invade Scotland.'

'Presumably not by the Scots?' Robert conjectured with a truculent grin.

'Some of them, anyway,' Cecil replied. 'They style themselves "The Lords of the Congregation" and they are united in their wish to see the Church in that nation governed by presbyteries, in defiance of Catholicism. They have converted the Earl of Arran, the former Protector and Regent of the French Queen Mary and he seeks our support to drive the French and all their ambitions out of Scotland. This would mean a friendly Protestant nation to our north and an end to the pernicious alliance between Scotland and France that has ever been a thorn in our side.'

'But Cecil also advises me that we have no money to raise an army,' Elizabeth added.

Robert's face broke into a broad smile. 'I would be honoured to raise a force in your name, my sweet, and allow my men to sack Edinburgh in order to reward themselves, thereby avoiding the need to pay them from the royal coffers.'

Cecil sighed. 'You are two hundred years too late for that, Robert. Our forebears may have conducted warfare in that manner, living off the conquered lands and bringing back plunder and hostages, but this will be a matter of State. A royal army commissioned in the Queen's name, bearing the battle banners of England and handing over any captured wealth to the Exchequer. How many men could you raise on those terms?'

'Whether it be a hundred, or thirty thousand,' Elizabeth asserted forcefully, 'he is not going. I forbid it!'

It fell silent as both men dealt with their embarrassment and it was Cecil who recovered first, when he remembered an earlier conversation in a hallway.

'If I might suggest the Duke of Norfolk, Your Majesty? He is Earl Marshall of England and your Lieutenant of the North. He has a sizeable following under his own livery and would be the most appropriate man to lead an army over the Scottish border in your name. I am tempted to add that should he lose his life in the process, then your Council would be rid of one of its more irritating members.'

Elizabeth smiled despite herself, leaving only Robert with a sour expression on his face as he saw the prospect of military glory slipping from his grasp.

'It shall be as you advise, Cecil,' Elizabeth announced. 'Have him commissioned without delay.'

'And what of me?' Robert asked petulantly.

Elizabeth reached out to grip his hand. 'You have duties closer to home, Robert, since I thought we might transfer to Windsor for a few days, from where we can organise a hunt. I am advised by the Chamberlain that Whitehall needs to be aired and sweetened, and since I have sent my Council to reflect on their impertinence over the matter of a royal marriage there is nothing to detain me here.'

For three months, from March to July of 1560, the English forces led by Thomas Howard laid siege to Leith. They seemed to be making little progress until they were greatly assisted by the death of Mary of Guise, in response to which the French seemed to lose heart and Howard was able to return home triumphant, bearing the English copy of the Treaty of Edinburgh, under which the French undertook to remove themselves from Scotland, which was henceforth to be governed by a Reformation Parliament in the name of its absentee Queen Mary. Scotland entered into a new peace treaty with England that was to replace the Auld Alliance with France and from this position of strength Elizabeth was able to secure, via her Ambassador in France Sir Nicholas Throckmorton, a further treaty of non-aggression with France itself.

Back in London for a brief family visit following his success in Paris, the English Ambassador to France, Nicholas Throckmorton, was invited to dinner with Cecil at his private house in The Strand.

'Thanks to you there will now be less French dishes served up in Edinburgh,' Cecil told him.

Throckmorton smiled. 'Indeed, I was at the Palais du Louvre when the French commanders came wandering back with their tails between their legs. I could tell from the general malaise around the Palace that the French had lost their enthusiasm for supporting Scotland and was by this means able to persuade them to accede to an end to the Auld Alliance.'

'For which the whole of England, and most importantly Her Majesty, will forever be in your debt,' Cecil acknowledged. 'But think you not that we might play the French at their own game?'

'Your meaning?'

'How strong is the Protestant faction in France?'

'Growing by the week, as more and more of those of the Calvinist belief flock into Paris to avoid persecution by the

Guise brothers in the more rural, and therefore Catholic, areas. They are known collectively as "Huguenots" and they have benefitted considerably from the more tolerant policies of that old battle-axe the Queen Dowager Catherine de Medici. It's all to do with the age-old feud between the Bourbons and the House of Lorraine, with which I will not bore you, but the Guise faction at the French Court — the irredeemable Catholics — have fallen somewhat from favour since the sister died in Edinburgh and the rival House of Bourbon has gained ascendency under Louis, Prince of Condé, who is a leading light of the Calvinist faith and therefore the Huguenot cause. But I see your eyes glazing over, my friend — do I proceed too quickly for you?'

'Indeed,' Cecil replied, 'it was like listening to one of my own perorations before the Privy Council. But do I take from what you have said that these Huguenots would benefit greatly from English support?'

'Undoubtedly, but do you propose to occupy Paris, as the French occupied Edinburgh?'

'Clearly not,' Cecil replied, 'but presumably, were England to supply money and perhaps a few closely disguised agents, into your control, this would assist the Huguenot cause and thereby further undermine the Catholic rule in France?'

'Without a doubt,' Throckmorton assured him.

'This House of Bourbon of which you speak,' Cecil continued, 'does it have within it any princes of the royal blood that we might consider as a husband for our own dear Queen?'

'There are the younger Valois brothers, Henry of Anjou and Francis of Alençon, whose brother Francis is currently King of France, with the Scots Mary as his consort. They are notional Catholics, but known to be tolerant of the Huguenots, if only in order that they may enjoy a quiet life.'

47

'So they would be unlikely to disapprove of Elizabeth's preference for religious tolerance?'

'Quite the opposite, my lord. They would applaud it. Do I detect that you wish me to sound out the possibility of marriage between one of these two princes and our own Queen?'

'If you could persuade either — or indeed both — of them to offer their hand in marriage to Elizabeth, then not only would it silence a few strident voices in Council, but it would serve as a further public insult to Philip of Spain, while perhaps hosing down the flames of passion between Elizabeth and another less suitable.'

'You speak of Robert Dudley?'

'Dear God, have the rumours even travelled across to France?' Cecil groaned.

Throckmorton shook his head. 'I heard it from my wife's Steward when I returned to visit her in her sickness. I regret that my intelligence service in France is not so well developed.'

'So you would also welcome further recruits into the web you must weave to support the Huguenot cause?'

'Indeed I would, my lord. Have you someone in mind?'

'I do, although it will be for you to train him in matters of subtle enquiry and underhand dealing. He has approached my office several times seeking preferment and he is both skilled in law and so steeped in the Protestant cause that he was forced to flee into exile in Switzerland on the accession of the late Queen Mary. He speaks many of the languages of Europe, including French. His name is Francis Walsingham.'

VI

Cecil sat staring, unseeing, through the open door to his temporary chamber on the ground floor of the State Apartments at Windsor Castle, where he seemed destined to spend many months due to another outbreak of plague in London. His brain was spinning with the implications of the news that had been brought to him of Amy Dudley's death, and the suggestion that Robert had pushed her down the stairs. The rumour was now ringing around the Castle like a fanfare. Robert Dudley had received the news privately via his Steward, Thomas Blount and had immediately gone into virtual seclusion at his house in Kew, refusing to receive even messengers from Cecil, such was reported to be his grief and anguish.

Whichever it was, and howsoever Amy Dudley had come to die, the consequences would be momentous. On the one hand, Cecil mused, his scheming to interest Elizabeth in the hand of some royal prince — and preferably a French one — would suffer a massive set-back now that her adored Robert was free to marry. Not only that, but if she continued to show him such favour, including his recent elevation to the Order of the Garter, his growing unpopularity might flare into rebellion, no doubt led by Thomas Howard, who Cecil could ill afford to oppose on Robert's behalf, given his proven and ongoing ability to raise an army.

But there was another, and darker, way of reading the situation. What if Amy had been killed by Robert, or at least on his order? What if his motivation had been to leave him free to marry Elizabeth and become her consort? Could either of the loving couple survive such a scandal, and might Robert not then be assassinated, either by someone who heartily detested him, or someone who thought it best for England and its reputation abroad, if Dudley were dead? And might his demise be skilfully linked with a rebellion against Elizabeth's reign by disaffected Catholics?

He looked up as a page appeared in his doorway, resplendent from head to foot in the royal livery. Cecil anticipated his message. 'You come from the Queen?'

'No, Master Secretary, from her Senior Lady Mistress Parry. She bids you attend upon her urgently and she is in the Withdrawing Chamber above.'

Cecil lost no time in answering the summons and found Blanche pacing backwards and forwards across the carpet, wringing her hands like a washerwoman and muttering something under her breath. As she caught sight of Cecil, she ran over to him and grabbed his hands pleadingly. 'Dearest cousin, what are we to do?' she moaned.

'Regarding what?'

'Have you not heard the dreadful tidings? Amy Dudley is dead, seemingly at the hand of another and rumour is rife that it was Robert's doing.'

'Where is your mistress?' Cecil asked sharply as he finally realised that they were alone.

Blanche jerked her head backwards. 'In her Bedchamber, bawling her eyes out. She will see no-one, not even me, and she refuses either food or drink.'

'That will assist no-one,' Cecil replied firmly. 'Go in there and bring her out.'

'I dare not, William — in her present humour she would have me hanged!'

'Then let us see if she'll put to death her Secretary of State,' Cecil replied as he strode towards the dividing door.

Blanche screamed at him to come back, just as the doorway in question filled to the sight of Elizabeth, her hair tousled and hanging loosely to her shoulders, dressed only in a long nightgown, red at the eyes and nose and with bare feet. She smiled weakly at Cecil. 'I will preserve you from the risk of losing your head, Master Secretary. And more to the point, I will also preserve my maidenly reputation from further ribald rumours regarding who enters my Bedchamber.'

Blanche gave a squawk of disapproval and squeezed past Elizabeth into the bedchamber, re-emerging seconds later with a long cloak that she draped over the nightgown and a pair of silver-embroidered pattens that she stooped to force onto Elizabeth's feet.

Cecil walked calmly towards Elizabeth, took one of her hands in his and led her towards the fire that had been lit three hours earlier. 'On this occasion I will not presume to pass comment on your late rising,' he jested lightly as he pressed her gently down into one of the padded chairs before the fire. 'I presume that the cause of your distress is the news regarding Amy Dudley?'

'What must I do, Cecil?' Elizabeth wailed pathetically. 'They are already laying the deed at Robert's door and how long before I am also implicated? Help me, Cecil!'

'Please calm yourself, my Lady,' Cecil murmured as reassuringly as he was able. 'I shall not leave a single stone unturned until I get to the truth of the matter ahead of anyone else, and I shall then mould whatever that truth may be into a suitable form that shall reflect nothing of guilt towards your good self.'

'I want the actual truth, Cecil, not whatever version of it you choose to broadcast abroad for public consumption. I must know if Robert did it for love of me, and if I shall be adjudged to be of equal guilt in consequence.'

'You cannot be held to account for whatever sickness of mind may have overtaken Robert,' Cecil assured her, 'and we do not know for certain that his hand was behind it. First and foremost there must be an inquest into the circumstances of the death, and regardless of its outcome I shall then conduct my own discreet further enquiries.'

Blanche looked up at Cecil with an expression of enquiry. 'You seek to ferret out the truth?'

'Her Majesty demands it. And I would know it for myself.'

'But surely those responsible will hide themselves away from your interrogations?' Elizabeth objected.

Blanche gave a light chuckle as she held Cecil's gaze. 'This will not be the first time that my cousin has gone in search of the truth by means of stealth. As when he was able to prove that there had been no letter passing between you and those implicated in the Wyatt rebellion against your sister. And later, whether or not your sister was indeed with child.'

Cecil allowed himself a slow smile. 'You mean Thomas Ashton?'

'Was that the wretched young man's name? A true rogue if ever there was one, but useful in wheedling the truth out of young female servants. Are you still in communication with him, William?'

'Why would I be, given his nature? The last I saw of him was when we returned him to his mother's estate of Knighton, on which occasion you were both present. For all I know he has spent his way through the family's modest fortune and is even now in gaol as the result of another of his devious schemes.

More charitably, he probably has three wives, six children and a burgeoning gut full of local ale and bacon.'

'But you will seek him out?' Elizabeth asked. 'He has been of good service to us before and there shall be rich reward should he be able to bring us the truth of this terrible business.'

'The rich reward will no doubt secure his services.' Cecil nodded. 'I shall journey into Leicestershire when his services are required.'

'Why not now?' Elizabeth demanded with irritation.

'Because, Your Majesty,' Cecil replied, 'I wish first to acquaint myself with as much of the facts as I am able. Only then shall I unleash my ferret.'

The inquest that Robert Dudley had insisted on in order to clear his name concluded that 'the lady Amy by misfortune came to her death and not otherwise.' But Cecil was far from satisfied, since 'misfortune' was apt to cover death by the hand of another. It was with Robert's blessing that Cecil pointed his mount's head north and on the morning of the fourth day found himself being admitted into the small ground floor chamber of the Manor of Knighton. He had been advised by the slovenly looking self-proclaimed Steward of the Manor that 'the master' was engaged in 'important business upstairs' and Cecil turned to the sound of footsteps descending the staircase that led to the upper chamber. There was a man in his early twenties who was barely recognisable as the Tom Ashton whom Cecil had carried in his memory for the past four years. He was now almost six feet in height, handsome in that ruddy-faced way common to country gentlemen and with a fashionably trimmed short black beard and moustache.

'They told me that I was being graced by a visit from the Queen's Secretary,' Tom grinned cheekily, 'but all I see before me is William Cecil.'

'One and the same, young Thomas,' Cecil assured him, 'although I fear that the years have been kinder to you than they have to me. I come on the Queen's business, but in secret.'

'From which I deduce that she has not sent you to collect those debts due by way of judgments imposed by her local bloodhound. In any case, you are too good to be employed as a bailiff. So what business of Her Majesty's brings you back into Leicestershire?'

'I have need of your services,' Cecil told him, 'and if my experienced eyes do not deceive me, you have need of the rich reward that Her Majesty is offering for those services. Have you heard of a Courtier called Robert Dudley?'

'The man who killed his wife in order to marry the Queen?'

'The man who stands so condemned in the estimate of the Court, certainly,' Cecil conceded, 'but it shall be your task to prove otherwise.'

'I am no file-tongued lawyer,' Tom objected.

Cecil nodded. 'Indeed you are not, but you are a very devious, underhand, unprincipled jackanapes whose capacity for eluding the gallows is matched only by your ability to tup information from female servants of the lower sort.'

'I would not quarrel with that description from an old friend such as yourself,' Tom said, 'but mind me not to seek a good name from you should I seek a position at Court.'

'I will also mind you not to ask for same,' Cecil said. 'Now, do you wish to learn the details of your mission?'

'How large is the "rich reward" of which you spoke?'

'How extensive are your debts?'

'I have in truth lost count of them,' Tom replied with an open and candid grin.

'You will undertake to weasel out the true circumstances of the death of Amy Dudley?'

'I will, once you give me such information as you have at present.'

'Very well, pay attention and listen carefully,' Cecil instructed him. 'The eighth of September last — a Sunday — was the day of the Abingdon Autumn Fair. Abingdon is in Berkshire, and close by the location of said fair is a mansion known as Cumnor Place. Living there on that day was Amy Dudley, Amy Robsart as was previously, the wife of Robert Dudley, but given to living separately from him. She was a long-term guest of the tenant of Cumnor, Sir Anthony Forster, and occupied most of the upper storey of the house, in which she had a suite of rooms. Also dwelling there at that time were Sir Anthony's wife and two other of his relatives, a Mrs Odingsells and a Mrs Owen. Amy Dudley kept a separate household, whose ten or so servants were accommodated in the old stables beneath the house. Leading between the two — the upper storey and the stables — was a staircase of some fifteen or so steps, by means of which one might access the rear garden. Do you wish me to repeat any of this?' Cecil asked as the sound of raised voices outside grew louder.

'I think not,' Tom assured him, 'but first I must silence that clamour.'

He rose from the table and walked outside, where his Steward was shouting the odds with three men armed with clubs, once of whom was claiming to be a county magistrate while another insisted that he was a shire constable.

'There you are!' the magistrate yelled. 'Come you outside to pay your debts, or shall you be consigned to the lock-up awaiting transport to Leicester Gaol?'

'Neither, you impudent oaf,' Tom replied heatedly. 'I have long since denied those debts, as you are well aware.'

'A pity, then, that you did not see fit to travel to deny them in my court. Take him in charge, Samuel Hopkins, and if he resists you may rattle his noggin.'

'Before you do anything of the sort,' came a commanding voice behind them as Cecil stepped out into the sunlight, 'how much is the full extent of the debt?'

'It runs to six shillings in all,' the magistrate told him, 'but what interest be it of yours?'

'This man is currently engaged on the Queen's business,' Cecil replied, 'and it would not be convenient for him to do so from a cell viewed through a grille set into the roadway of a street in Leicester.'

'What about the six shillings?' the magistrate demanded. 'I am authorised by Her Majesty to uphold the law in this county. And who, while we are about it, might you be?'

'I am William Cecil, Secretary of State for England and I am authorised by Her Majesty to enact the law for the entire nation,' Cecil replied calmly as he reached into the money purse at his belt, selected six shillings and threw it down onto the well-trodden earth between them. 'There's your money — now leave us in peace.'

'That was very generous of you,' Tom said as they sat back down again. 'I am eternally in your debt.'

'Not eternally,' Cecil replied, 'since I shall reimburse myself from whatever sum Her Majesty authorises me to pay you for your services. Now how much, if anything, do you recall from our interrupted discussion?'

Tom closed his eyes and thought hard before replying.

'A country house somewhere — a lady living in an upper storey reached by a set of stairs that led up from a garden. And something about a local fair. Will that suffice?'

'For the moment,' Cecil nodded, 'but now to the gravamen of the matter. The lady in question was of course Amy Dudley and she was found at the foot of the stairs with her neck broken and therefore dead. The person who found her was one of the kitchen staff employed at the house, a girl called Lucy Bracegirdle and with her was a young man from nearby Abingdon with whom she planned to go to it in the stables where she lived. They called in the authorities. There was nothing seen of any other person near the body, nor anything to suggest how it might have come to be there. Everyone else in the house was at the fair. '

'What said the authorities?' Tom asked.

Cecil's face set slightly. 'Therein lies the object of your mission. There was a coroner's inquest that concluded that Amy Dudley died as the result of "misfortune" and I wish you to probe deeper into what precisely that "misfortune" might have been.'

'Surely the word is apt to suggest that the lady fell accidentally?'

'It is also apt to suggest that someone pushed her,' Cecil pointed out.

'Her husband?'

'Him, or someone at his bidding. The man himself was with the Queen at Windsor Palace.'

Tom's face set in a look of concentration, then he had a further question. 'If there can be no proof of Dudley's involvement, why is there any ongoing problem?'

'Because popular ill-feeling towards him also shouts loudly that the absence of any evidence of his involvement does not mean that he was not involved.'

'You talk in riddles, Master Cecil. You say that absence of proof of guilt does not eliminate suspicion of guilt?'

'Precisely, which is why your services are required — to prove that he was not involved.'

'I must prove a negative assertion?'

'In the sense you mean, yes. But there is one other piece of information that you do not currently possess.'

'And that is?'

'The position of the head-dress.'

'What of it?'

'It was found on her head. Picture that in your mind for a moment, then tell me what that suggests to you.'

Tom's eyes opened wide as the penny dropped. 'If she fell from a height and landed sufficiently hard to break her neck, her head adornment, whatever it was, would have fallen from her head.'

'Precisely and the fact that it did not adds fuel to the speculation that she was hit from behind. There were several bruises on her head and it is possible that these were the first blows, until the one that broke the neck. She slid to the ground and her coif hood remained in place. This is a more likely explanation than that she fell down a set of stairs, fifteen in number, then hit the ground.'

'So I am to travel to this place and ask questions regarding the positioning of the hood, beginning with the girl who found her, who by your account is receptive to a good seeing to?'

Cecil winced. 'Precisely. I can hardly be expected to conduct such an enquiry, given that I am known to be a favoured Courtier of both the Queen and the man who she would marry if given her head.'

'And given that you are an old man who would not be likely to attract the passion of a kitchen wench?'

'Less of your impertinence. Prepare to ride south with me on the morrow and look to it that you do not fail me. The future of the nation may depend upon your disgraceful carnal talents.'

VII

William Cecil was no sooner back in London, after dispatching Tom off to Cumnor Place, than his son Robert brought him news of another dramatic development. King Francis II of France had died a few weeks short of his seventeenth birthday, of a malady that some said was an infection of the ear that had travelled to his brain and others put down to poison, depending upon one's religious affiliations. The consequence, whatever the cause, was that Queen Dowager Catherine de Medici was now Regent for Francis's successor, his ten-year-old brother Charles, who was destined to become Charles IX in due course. The old Queen had never been a great admirer of her Scottish daughter-in-law and before long — according to Throckmorton's information, diligently acquired from sources corrupted by his new assistant Walsingham — England could expect Mary back in Scotland, aged a mere eighteen, highly eligible as a bride and anxious to bolster Catholic fortunes following the death of her mother Mary of Guise, even though the most influential person within the rival Protestant ruling faction was her own brother James Stuart, her father's illegitimate offspring.

England had benefitted greatly from the brief period of peace across its northern borders following the tearing up of the Auld Alliance and the dominance within Scotland of the Presbyterian Church that could, if one glibly skipped points of difference, be regarded as roughly equivalent to the English Church of which Elizabeth was the guiding light. The last thing England needed was for Mary to make a powerful match with a Catholic prince, particularly one who was either Spanish or affiliated in some way with the Habsburg Empire.

It was time to take a deep breath, summon up the moral courage and raise once again the matter of a royal marriage with Elizabeth, who had successfully avoided the topic for almost two years now and who, if one believed prurient tittle-tattle, continued to lie on most nights with Robert Dudley. The worrying factor in such gossip was that it tended to originate with the more humble domestic staff within the royal household and therefore the most likely to be aware of its accuracy. One did not need a great deal of experience in bed-making to know whether one pillow or two had been engaged.

The sooner that Elizabeth was married off the better, since experience had demonstrated that rumours of Robert's involvement in the death of his wife was not likely to act as a damper on their passion for each other. Since whoever was eventually chosen as her husband would clearly be regarded by Elizabeth as second best, one could select candidates on the basis of their significance for the role of England within Europe, with particular reference to blocking any aggrandisement of Spain. This left two possible candidates, neither of whom would be likely to appeal to Elizabeth and Cecil felt his bowels knot as he contemplated the prospect of pressing their claims on her.

First and foremost, from England's perspective, came Archduke Charles of Austria, whose name had already been whispered in Elizabeth's disinterested ear. He was the son of the current Holy Roman Emperor and would be a powerful block against Philip of Spain. He would also make a very dangerous suitor for Mary of Scotland, from England's perspective, since Charles was a practising Catholic.

But recent events in France had revealed two other possible candidates for the role of Queen's Consort. The French King in Regency, Charles of Valois-Orleans-Angouleme, had two younger brothers who were currently unmarried. The first and the older of the two, was Henri, Duke of Angouleme, their mother's favourite and an artistically inclined Protestant. A match with the royal house of France would sit very nicely with England's need to show Spain that it had powerful friends, and Cecil hoped that Elizabeth would be attracted to a man eighteen years her junior who was known to be inclined towards scholarship and the arts rather than warfare.

Elizabeth tutted with irritation when Cecil raised the matter tentatively during a late supper, after she had returned from a day's hunting with Robert in the grounds of her favoured deer park at Richmond and Robert had tactfully withdrawn to his house in Kew.

'Do you intend to ruin this excellent supper with more unwanted advice on who I should marry?' she demanded. 'You grow as tedious as my Council, which is why I have sent them away to reflect on their presumption. Take care that I do not do the same to you, Cecil, for all the years that you have served me loyally and well. Why can none of you accept that there is every chance that I will never marry? And please do not incur my displeasure by making yet another reference to the need for a royal heir — as I understand it, I can nominate my own heir, just as my brother Edward did.'

Cecil braced himself to give the obvious advice. 'Forgive me for my temerity, Your Majesty, but I am duty-bound to remind you of the chaos into which the nation was plunged as the result of the crown being bequeathed to the Grey girl.'

'Enough of this, Cecil! When do you expect to be able to bring me further news regarding the death of Robert's wife?'

'Whenever Thomas Ashton returns, my Lady.'

'If prefer "Your Majesty" while you are presuming to advise me, Cecil. And what of my Scottish cousin?'

'My informants advise that she is feeling some discomfort in her present role as the second Queen Dowager in France, with the first one — her late husband's mother — now spreading stories that her precious Francis died as the result of his over-exertions with his young and beautiful Queen. It is believed that she will return to Scotland to take up her crown there.'

'Will she be welcome, think you?'

'Not if she attempts to return the nation to the Catholic observances, certainly, and therein the importance of what I had hoped to raise with you this evening. Mary of Scotland is still young and beautiful, so they say, and will no doubt be seeking another husband from among the princes of Europe. I had hoped that you might take your pick of them first.'

'You venture out onto thin ice again, Cecil. I will marry when, where — and more to the point — whomsoever I choose. You have never yet suggested an Englishman for my husband and yet I seem to recall that when my late sister announced her intention of marrying a Spaniard her Council were at great pains to suggest English alternatives. Have we run out of suitable partners for my marriage bed on this side of the Channel?'

'Forgive me, but I believe that Your Majesty may already have one in mind.'

'Silence on that, Cecil, if you wish to finish your supper! We will discuss this again when you bring me news from Thomas Ashton.'

Tom extracted the long piece of string from his tunic and made as much noise as possible stomping up and down the narrow wooden staircase that led to the upper chambers of Cumnor Place. A quick glance through the gap between two of the planks confirmed that his objective had been achieved; there was now a young woman of approximately his own age gazing up at his legs below the knee of his tunic.

'What d'yer think yer think yer up ter?' the girl demanded.

Tom made a big display of drawing the string across the width of the stairs before he looked down to answer her. 'These stairs are dangerous, and I'm hoping to get the commission to replace them. For the time being I'm just measuring to see how much wood will be required. Is your master at home?'

'Them's all at church, it bein' Sunday, so yer picked the wrong day. Anyroad, old Jacob Boxmore does the carpenter work around 'ere, so yer wastin' yer time twice. Pity, all the same, since yer better lookin' than old Jacob. I'm Lucy, by the way.'

'Thomas,' he replied with another pointed look down the top of her bodice. 'So what do you do around here?'

'I works in the scullery.'

'So what makes you think that there's nothing wrong with the stairs? I was told that a lady fell down them a year or so past.'

'She didn't fall 'cos of any accident,' Lucy assured him. 'She took a dive, ter put an end to 'er miserable life.'

'And how do you know that?' Tom challenged her as he came back down the stairs.

'Everyone round the 'ouse could tell yer,' Lucy replied with her eyes fixed on his groin. 'She 'ad this 'ere painful lump in one've 'er titties and some days we could 'ear 'er upstairs, cryin' wi' the pain. Then 'er 'usband ran off wi' the Queen, or so they reckons, an' on the day she done it she sent the 'ole 'ouse'old off ter the fair, so's she could be alone ter do 'erself in. I were the one what found 'er, just sorta lyin' there, wi' 'er 'ead lyin' a funny way. It were 'orrible.'

'I heard that she still had her bonnet on her head,' Tom said, 'so how could she have fallen all that way down and not lost her headgear?'

'That were me,' Lucy confessed.

'What do you mean, exactly?'

'Well, like I said, 'er 'ead were all lyin' a funny way, an' she didn't look proper dignified. 'Er bonnet thing were lyin' ter one side, so I just popped it back on 'er 'ead, ter make 'er look a bit more decent. Yer won't tell no-one, will yer?'

'Of course not,' Tom assured her.

'You are certain of this?' Cecil asked once Tom had recounted what he had learned from Lucy Bracegirdle. 'You had no reason to doubt what she said?'

'None whatsoever. And it has the ring of truth about it, does it not? Talking of rings, there is a certain young lady in Knighton to whom I promised myself in marriage. One of several, as it transpires, but this particular one has a brother who is twice my size and who has taken unkindly to my attentions towards his sister. May I hide here in London with you until he has forgotten where he has hidden his sword?'

'What of your mother?' Cecil asked. 'I did not see her while at Knighton; is she with your sister in that place near Nottingham?'

Tom shook his head. 'She died of an ague last winter. As for Grace, she's a happy blacksmith's wife in Attenborough and expecting her fourth.'

Cecil thought for a moment. 'You may not reside in this house, since I still have troubled memories of the chaos into which you launched it during your previous lodging here. But I will employ you as a clerk upon the many matters that now cross my desk in the course of my duties as Master Secretary and you may find cheap lodgings in the city. Given your unfathomable power over the fairer sex, you may even find a pliant landlady who will allow you to lodge between her thighs as the price of your bed and board.'

'I hear that your son Robert is now your Senior Clerk.'

'Yes, and now, if you annoy him as you once did, he has men about him who would think nothing of putting you in the gutter, so leave well alone. Take yourself off and ruin the Cook's day by advising her that you are to be fed ere you seek lodgings and for preference a good league from here.'

'Will you be joining me for supper?'

'No, I have need to advise the Queen of what you have discovered and she will no doubt give me my supper while I sing her a song. Now off with you.'

'How good is this information?' Elizabeth asked eagerly as she beckoned Cecil and Blanche over.

'It comes from Thomas Ashton and he may be relied upon.'

'I dread to think how he obtained it,' Blanche sniffed disapprovingly. 'No doubt from some innocent wench he cruelly seduced with his oily charm.'

'Not so innocent, by his account,' Cecil said, 'but reliable nevertheless. She was the girl who discovered Amy Dudley's body and who can attest that the circumstances are suggestive that the lady took her own life.'

'So Robert really was innocent of her death?' Elizabeth said, 'and how much should we reward this young man who brings us the reassurance?'

'Not so much that he may set himself up as a gentleman of leisure,' Cecil replied, 'since I need to retain him in my service in anticipation of further need of information from low quarters. Let us say fifty pounds.'

'No doubt to be spent on whores,' Blanche muttered as she carved herself a thin slice of cold pork.

'Enough, Blanche,' Elizabeth admonished her. 'Whatever his morals he has brought us great comfort. Does Robert know yet?' she asked of Cecil, who shook his head.

'No, my Lady. I heard that he was in Plymouth on your behalf.'

'He is in Plymouth, certainly, but I suspect that his pretence at organising my navy conceals a desire for personal wealth.'

'The two may happily co-exist, my Lady,' Cecil told her, 'since those merchants who put to sea in these perilous times must be armed against privateers and Spanish aggressors. The cannon that they load below decks may be used in England's cause, should the need arise.'

'Talking of which, how go matters in France and the Low Countries?' Elizabeth asked.

'I have a new man installed in Paris, working with your Ambassador Throckmorton. He reports that the tensions between Catholic and Huguenot are as strong as ever, which should keep their boy-King well occupied. Your cousin Mary is reported to be packing her bags to return to Scotland and I must place a man in Edinburgh to see how she is received by her own subjects when she does.'

VIII

Word came to Cecil that the Queen was laid up in her bed with a fever, interspersed with frequent vomiting. He hastened up to the Audience Chamber and Blanche Parry scuttled in when advised that he was asking for her.

'How goes your mistress?' he asked.

Blanche shook her head in a gesture of uncertainty. 'It may have been a bad oyster, but pray God that nobody has sought to poison her. The kitchens are being inspected for rats and Robert's favoured physician is with her as we speak. She is purging badly and has dismissed all of her Ladies but me.'

'Do you not fear infection yourself?'

'Of course, but what like of friend would I be to desert her when she has most need of comfort? Pray God that Master Lopez can tell us more,' she added as the man in question came through the door from the adjoining Withdrawing Chamber, which was being kept locked and guarded as an additional precaution against the transmission of further infection in either direction.

Lopez had a solemn face as he bowed and Blanche eagerly sought his diagnosis. 'I fear it may be the smallpox, Mistress, but we shall only know for certain when — and of course if — the blisters show themselves.'

'Could she die of it?' Cecil asked.

Lopez nodded. 'Many people do, but given her otherwise robust constitution there is hope. She is asking for you both.'

Blanche caught the fearful look on Cecil's face and reached out to place a reassuring hand on the sleeve of his Court gown.

'I will go in there again, cousin. Do you remain here and I will bring word of her wishes.'

Ten minutes later, Blanche came back into the Audience Chamber that Cecil had been crossing backwards and forwards in his nervousness, wiping tears from her eyes.

'She fears to die and is insistent that you summon Council and have Robert appointed Protector of the Realm should that be her fate. As to any heir, she refuses to appoint one, but muttered that if the Council were fool enough to offer her crown to Mary of Scotland, then at least it would remain on a Tudor head.'

'Where is Robert?' Cecil asked as he realised with a start that the man closest to Elizabeth's heart at this perilous time was not already in attendance.

'Back in Plymouth, or so he claimed as his intended destination when he rode away in a high dudgeon three days ago. I have sent messengers after him.'

'I will of course summon Council,' Cecil assured her, 'and do you see to your mistress, with deepest prayers from myself for her complete recovery.'

'If it be the smallpox,' Blanche replied ominously, 'she may not wish to recover. She was ever vain of her beauty.'

Three days later Blanche shuddered as she looked down at Elizabeth's blistered face, assured her that the worst of her illness was over and rushed out to give urgent instructions that the Queen was to be allowed no mirror, or any other object in which she might see her reflection.

In Council, Cecil's announcement that Her Majesty had given him a stern command that in the event of her death Robert Dudley was to be appointed Protector of the Realm was treated with howls of derision and more than one vulgar noise.

'It is only to be brought to pass should she die,' he explained above the excited hubbub that followed.

'And the heir?' Thomas Howard demanded. 'Is it to be the Scots Mary?'

'She has left that matter to Council,' Cecil replied, 'but I would strongly advise against such a choice, if England is to remain Protestant.'

'It has not thrived whilst in that Godless state,' Howard replied with a surly grimace. 'And we are surrounded by stronger nations that are Catholic in their observances — what chance England should Elizabeth die, leaving us defenceless?'

'She is but one woman,' Cecil reminded him, 'and a woman, what is more, who relies upon this collection of sour ingrates to assist her in devising the best policies for the nation she has inherited. I may advise you privily that she had no wish to become Queen and has put all thoughts of personal happiness aside while she gives her all for her people.'

'Although she reserves a small part of it for one of them,' Howard sneered, to resulting sniggers among those who followed his lead.

Cecil went white with anger as he turned his head sharply in Howard's direction. 'Would you have let slip that unworthy remark had Her Majesty been among us?' he challenged him and Howard's eyes dropped to the table. 'Well, gentlemen,' Cecil said brusquely, 'is the Queen to be obeyed in what may well be her dying wish? Do we advise Dudley that he must prepare to be Lord Protector?'

'You'll have to find him first,' someone reminded the company.

Howard was determined to have the last word. 'It is put about that he is in Plymouth on the Queen's business. But curiously, I hear tell that he journeyed by way of Chartley.'

Cecil was not greatly comforted even when Council agreed to Elizabeth's wish. Chartley was the family home of Viscount Hereford and his wife Lettice Knollys, one of the Queen's Ladies. Those Ladies had been sent home during Elizabeth's illness and Viscount Hereford was on military duty in Ireland.

Four days later Blanche could hear Elizabeth's screams as she raced up the staircase from the kitchens. Blanche took one look at the scene before her eyes and cursed whichever fool had disobeyed, or forgotten, her stern instruction. Elizabeth was sitting bolt upright in bed, gazing at her reflection in the polished base of a serving dish that had, earlier that day, contained a handful of her favourite sugared almonds. She was rubbing furiously at her face as the screams subsided into anguished sobs and she gazed helplessly back at Blanche as her old friend pulled her hands from her face.

'You must not attack them, my Lady. They will go down once the liquid drains from them — you'll see!'

Elizabeth's face was a mass of dark blood blisters, each filled with a faintly unpleasant-smelling liquid. There had been no doubt for some days that the malady that had afflicted the Queen had been smallpox, but none dared tell her, and despite every effort on Blanche's part, her mistress had now seen the ugliness for herself.

'These eruptions — they will leave scars, will they not?'

'They certainly will if you rub or scratch them,' Blanche replied in a tone of voice more appropriate for a mother with a child. 'But it affects each person differently and at least you are alive.'

'But what manner of spectacle will I present to my people?' Elizabeth wailed. 'And if Robert should see me like this — do not grant him admission, I beg you!'

'He is in Plymouth, my Lady, although I sent fast messengers when it was thought that you might die. Council agreed to his Protectorship.'

It fell silent while Blanche made a great display of fussing round the bedclothes, gently removing the serving dish from Elizabeth's hand in the process. Finally, when Elizabeth spoke again, it was in a flat tone of resignation. 'If I am not destined to die, but must face the world looking like a toad, is there not some preparation that will hide the scars when they form?'

'There is always the ceruse favoured by the more fashionable Ladies at Court,' Blanche reminded her. 'You have disdained to wear it in the past, content with your own peach-like complexion, but a white skin is accounted fashionable and ceruse is widely available. Do you wish me to acquire some for you?'

'My "peach-like complexion" is gone, Blanche,' Elizabeth moaned, 'to be replaced by a skin not unlike a pitted pear, like poor Viscountess Melton. See to it that I have ceruse to hand before I venture forth again and tell Robert, when he returns, that he is forbidden the presence because the young girl of his passionate youth is now an old crone with all the allure of a newt.'

Blanche sighed heavily and bowed backwards out of the presence. This was going to demand all the patience and diplomacy of which she was capable.

When Robert Dudley returned a week later, he glared defiantly back at Blanche as she barred his way into the Withdrawing Chamber.

'It is not just you, Robert. She has given firm instruction that no-one is allowed at her bedside at this time other than myself, her servers and Master Cecil. The governance of the realm must continue, hence Master Cecil's permitted audience, give his importance to the nation and his constant attention to the business of State.'

'But I have matters of great moment to impart,' Robert protested. 'Master Hawkins has set sail with three of his ships, partly paid for by the Queen's gold, and when they return we anticipate that the investment will be rewarded tenfold. His vessels are also armed and if Her Majesty can be persuaded to finance more of the same, it will not only secure a fortune for the Exchequer, but it will give the Spanish cause to hesitate before they attack our shores.'

Blanche smiled politely. 'Important though those matters are, they cannot compare with those issues that my Lady has to discuss with Master Cecil. God be praised that there is no further risk of death, but that prospect has sharpened her mind towards the future of the realm. Did you know that she and Cecil persuaded Council that were she to die, you were to be Lord Protector of England until the succession was decided?'

'See?' Robert replied triumphantly. 'If I am that important to the nation, then surely I am entitled to the same audience as Cecil? That is before we come to consider what claim I may have on her heart.'

Blanche could see no way around that argument, but she was still determined to protect her lifelong friend and she knew how she would feel in her predicament. 'Come back after dinner,' she suggested, 'and I will see what I can negotiate on your behalf.'

Robert appeared to be about to argue, but instead he thanked her, bowed and took his leave. Blanche instructed the pages to let no-one else into the Audience Chamber, then scuttled away in search of wardrobe attendants.

When Robert returned, he found Elizabeth seated in the Audience Chamber, propped up by cushions in a padded chair and seated behind a small desk. He would not have recognised her, had it not been for the fact that she was seated next to Blanche Parry and as he gazed somewhat quizzically at the whitened face, rouge-tinted cheeks and red ochre lips painted in the 'bow' style so favoured by fashionable ladies at Court, she held out her hand to be kissed.

'Thank God that you survived the sickness,' was all that Robert could manage as he stared, appalled, at the almost mocking substitute for Elizabeth's natural beauty — this false face that left her resembling an ageing whore.

'For all that you attended me during that time,' Elizabeth chided him, 'I could have died.'

Robert took her hand and kissed it, averting his eyes from her face. 'I rode back hard from Plymouth, where I have invested your gold in a venture that will repay you tenfold and will enable us to build and arm many more ships of the line.'

'We will soon be able to rival Spain?' Elizabeth asked eagerly.

Robert nodded. 'It wants only the ships — we have navigators enough and soon they will return to our shores loaded with riches.'

'This is well done,' Elizabeth replied, 'but I grow tired. Return on the morrow and we will take supper together while you delight me with further detail.'

As Robert bowed and turned towards the chamber door, he saw Cecil waiting quietly to approach the presence. He called back accusingly at Elizabeth, 'Tired or no, I doubt not that this man will be allowed longer audience.'

He swept from the chamber and Cecil advanced and tried to ignore the almost comical appearance of the lady he had served for over twenty years, to which Blanche had alerted him in advance. Having kissed the proffered hand, he smiled.

'It is so good to see Your Majesty restored to good health.'

'Good health perhaps, Cecil, but hardly good looks,' Elizabeth snapped back curtly. 'On which subject, pray advise my Council that I am unable to attend while I may still be at risk of passing my affliction to them. I have no doubt that they will be only too pleased to hear that. But I have in mind appointing another to assist you in resisting the wilder proposals of my more addle-brained Councillors, most notably Norfolk, who seems to think that the nation belongs to him by ancient right.'

'Majesty?'

'I wish to appoint a new Privy Councillor, Cecil,' Elizabeth repeated grumpily. 'Have I grown indistinct of speech, as well as ugly of appearance?'

'Far from it, Your Majesty, in either of those particulars. I merely await your instruction as to who the new Councillor might be.'

'You passed him on your way in.'

'Robert Dudley?'

'And why not? He is serving the nation well in the matter of increasing its navy, which we may well need if we are to transport men and arms across the sea to assist the Dutch in throwing the Spanish off their lands.'

'But...'

'But what, Cecil?'

'Robert is not the most popular man at Court, Your Majesty.'

'He is with me, and I have other plans for him.'

'May I share in Your Majesty's intentions?'

'Indeed you may, Cecil, since it will fall to you to implement them. In my current hag-like state, it is unlikely that even the oldest and ugliest prince in Europe would consider sharing a marriage bed with me, so we must look to some other means of securing alliances, and preferably with France or Scotland. Since the two are connected in the person of my cousin Mary, we must find a husband for her and preferably an English noble who may divert her from her Catholic ways. The chosen person will be King Consort of Scotland and well placed, through Mary's French associations, to approach France for a treaty of perpetual peace and mutual assistance in times of foreign aggression, which for England means from Spain.'

'An excellent ruse, Your Majesty,' Cecil replied, despite his misgivings, 'but at this moment I cannot think of such a nobleman in England.'

'Then we must create one, must we not? Now that he is to become a member of my Privy Council, it is fitting that Robert be ennobled. Which titles are currently available?'

Despite his shock at this proposal, Cecil knew the English nobility like the back of his hand. 'There is the vacant Earldom of Leicester, my Lady —'

'Your Majesty!' Elizabeth snapped. 'See to it, Cecil. Robert shall become Earl of Leicester, and shall be offered as a husband to Mary of Scotland.'

'But ... that is ... forgive me, but do you not wish him for yourself?'

'Of course I do, Cecil, but I love him too deeply to condemn him to wake up each day to the sight of me, with a complexion like a toad's arse. He must be ennobled and married off to the Scottish baggage. That is my command. Now leave me, ere the bounds of friendship be exceeded.'

Cecil bowed and walked sadly from the chamber. He was only a few yards down the hallway when he heard a sibilant hiss behind him and turned. Blanche came scurrying down the hall after him and grabbed his arm as she looked furtively behind her, then whispered urgently, 'Do not be disheartened by her manner towards you, cousin. In truth she is much distressed regarding her loss of beauty and she has a toothache besides, no doubt brought on by eating all those sweetmeats of which she is so fond. We must bend our heads against the storm and hope for fair weather in due course.'

'But in the meantime, must I carry out her commands?'

'It were best that you do, William, for in her present mood it would mean the Tower for you, were you to disobey. And now I must get back inside there, for another morning of ill-tempered instructions. Wish me luck.'

Cecil watched her retreating towards the Audience Chamber and felt pity for her. And for the nation, if it was to continue like this. He could only hope that Elizabeth had not lost her wits as well as her looks.

IX

'You do me great honour,' Robert murmured as he put down his eating knife in order to place his hand affectionately over Elizabeth's as they sat at supper. She gently slid her hand from under his, in a silent indication that the familiarity was not welcome, and reached across the board for an almond glazed in honey.

'The title of Earl of Leicester has been bestowed upon worthy predecessors,' she said. 'It was once held by Simon de Montfort and after him John of Gaunt. They were both great Englishmen and I hold you in the same regard, Robert.'

'Why my sudden preferment?' he asked nervously. 'Must I trade it for a place in your heart?'

'Enough talk of that,' Elizabeth pouted, 'since it can only be in mockery. The fresh-faced young girl you once embraced in the coppice at Hatfield has become a pock-marked old woman.'

'I can still look into your face and see that beauty,' Robert insisted, 'and in any case it is the woman within who has captured my love forever.'

'Dissemblance,' Elizabeth muttered as she felt her cheeks glow with exhilaration. 'With the title come many estates, including Kenilworth, which I seem to recall once belonged to your father,' she told him.

Robert's face set in disdain. 'Before he was executed by your wicked sister. Since then I am advised that it has become a ruin and will cost many thousands of pounds to restore.'

'You are in danger of forgetting that I too suffered under my sister's vile rule,' Elizabeth reminded him. 'She all but blamed me for the many challenges to her throne, one of which of course came from the Dudleys, who sought to place your brother's wife, the Lady Jane, in Mary's place.'

'We neither of us need to remind ourselves of those terrible days, and how — at our lowest ebb — we were allowed to meet in the Tower. I shall never forget how my heart leapt to see you again in all your natural fresh beauty.'

'Tosh, Robert,' Elizabeth murmured. 'I resembled a drowned rat, wearing a prison gown that clung to me with my own sweat. That said, I would happily resume that state, were I able to rid myself of this dreadful curse on my face.'

Without warning Robert leaned in sharply and kissed her cheek before she could recoil. Tears began to well in her eyes as she looked at him severely through the light mist that they formed over her vision. 'Must you torture me in this way, dearest Robert? I know I am hideous to view, yet you persist in assuring me that I still have your heart.'

'Still and forever,' Robert murmured as he leaned in again.

This time Elizabeth was prepared and she pulled back. 'You mentioned the cost of restoring Kenilworth. Shall you require a loan from my Treasury?'

'No, but thank you anyway for that generous offer,' Robert said. 'The wealth I expect to acquire from Master Hawkins's voyages will be more than sufficient, as you shall learn when your own investment is returned tenfold.'

'Where does he journey?'

'To the far southern ocean, where he will load slaves to carry across to the Indies. Then he will sell the slaves for gold, sugar and spices and speed back under a westerly to realise his fortune. And ours, of course.'

'Can such a fortune be carried in only one vessel?'

'There are three of them, a second one commanded by his cousin, a man called Francis Drake, who has ambitions to journey across the world to discover new lands and riches. We should offer to finance his venture, I suggest, since while he is conquering the ocean he will be showing the Spaniards that Englishmen are the superior sailors.'

It fell quiet, but Elizabeth still had the most important task ahead of her. 'How much do you love England, Robert?'

'Not as much as I love you.'

'Aren't they one and the same? While you prove your love for the nation, you demonstrate your love for its Queen, do you not?'

'Then there must be many who love you dearly,' Robert said.

'So I believe, and I thank God each day for the love shown to me by my people. But from some I must ask more. Those who are best placed to assist England must bear the greater burden.'

'What is it you seek from me, to prove my love, as if I had not shown it a thousand times already?'

'I wish you to journey to Scotland.'

'At the head of an army? You have but to command.'

'Not with an army, dearest Robert. A few armed men, perhaps, to ensure your safety.'

'As an envoy, then?'

'Yes, in a very important sense. Mary of Scotland must be wed to an English lord, in order to secure a lasting peace, both with that nation and with France, that together we may with safety seek to free the Low Countries of the Spanish yoke.'

'And you wish me to negotiate the peace terms that shall follow upon such a match?'

'We can leave that to Cecil, I believe.'

'I was about to mention him,' Robert replied. 'Why do you seek to send me in his stead? Why must I venture ahead of him, then leave the detailed peace treaty for him to hammer out?'

'Because of the delicate nature of the preliminaries. The English lord who is to be proposed as a bride for Mary must be a high-ranking Protestant I can trust.'

'Clearly. Who have you in mind?'

'Yourself, Robert.'

The sudden chill in the atmosphere was palpable, as Robert's eyes opened wide in amazement and his jaw dropped in disbelief. Elizabeth's eyes took on a pleading look as they stared each other out for a full minute, then Robert dropped his eyes to the damask cloth.

'You insult me, madam. Not only do you insult me, but you reject the love I have always offered to you with an innocence which I never thought you would betray. Now you seek to use me as a pawn in your ambition to silence the French whore for good. Well, hear this, Elizabeth of England. I will face a thousand enemy swords single-handed, I will sail across storm-tossed seas to discover new lands and riches for England, and I will lay down my life on the block should it be necessary to defend yours. All of this I will do for England. But for its Queen I will ever hold the flame of passion aloft, awaiting the day when she finally consents to be mine. Yet never, never, ever will I sully that love by wedding another. Of that you may rest assured. And so I seek your gracious leave to withdraw — the night has suddenly become chilly in my heart.'

Without waiting for leave to be granted he rose from the table, gave a stiff bow and walked swiftly to the chamber door while Elizabeth was seeking the words with which to frame an appropriate reply. She had thought of none by the time that the doors closed behind Robert's departing figure and she let out a long animal howl of anguish and self-pity.

Behind the arras beyond the half-open door, Blanche Parry deemed the moment appropriate to withdraw. She had, as requested, been listening for any verbal signal from her mistress that she should enter the chamber and put a stop to whatever inappropriateness might be taking place. But she had also promised her cousin Cecil to act as his eyes and ears and she had a good deal of which to warn him.

'He said all that?' Cecil asked disbelievingly as Blanche reported the conversation to him the following morning. 'I have never known the popinjay be so gifted with the English language.'

'I may have misremembered some of the actual words,' Blanche admitted with a frown, 'but the sentiment was unmistakable. He will not do it.'

'We shall see about that,' Cecil replied. 'Once I have everything in place and can so advise Her Majesty, she will have his head if he still refuses.'

'She would not take Robert's head, surely?'

'Would she not? Have you not noticed the change in her since her illness? And you her closest companion?'

'What do you mean?'

'Before she fell sick, she could always rely upon her belief in her own beauty to win men's hearts to her bidding, like a simple country wench will employ her art and charms to hook herself a local squire. Now she feels that God has betrayed her, pitting her face with those unseemly scars. She is angry at God, bitter within herself and determined to rule by sheer fear and force of personality, if need be. If I judge her aright, any refusal by Robert to do her bidding will twist in her breast like an assassin's dagger. She still loves him, but fears that he can no longer bear to look upon her. You are a woman — how would you feel if thus placed?'

'I am over fifty years of age, cousin,' Blanche replied, 'and no man ever showed the same devotion to me that Robert has poured upon my mistress, so I cannot judge. But of this I can assure you — Robert forswears to do her bidding and you will have a mountain to climb to change his mind, even should the Scots Mary be willing.'

'We shall see, cousin, we shall see,' Cecil said confidently as he led her gently by the hand through the door of his inner chamber, in a polite indication that their meeting was over. As he walked back through the outer chamber, he called out to Tom Ashton. 'Tom, seek out a man called Thomas Randolph, who resides in Thames Street somewhere. Bring him back with you, then remain with us for the conversation that will follow.'

Two hours later Thomas Randolph, who had, on Cecil's bidding, made covert contact with the Earl of Arran, one of the leaders of the Protestant faction in Scotland, was seated in front of Cecil, with Tom Ashton perching on a stool to the side.

'Randolph,' Cecil said warmly once the introductory pleasantries were out of the way, 'are you still in communication with the Scottish Earl James Hamilton?'

'The Earl of Arran? Why yes,' Randolph replied.

'And how go matters for Protestants in his country?'

Randolph shrugged his shoulders in a gesture of indecision. 'Middling well, although they are apprehensive that once Mary has established her rule more firmly, she will lead her people by the nose back to Rome.'

'So they would welcome the prospect of her becoming heavily influenced by an English noble of strong Protestant persuasion?'

'Undoubtedly, but it is to be questioned whether she would listen to Arran himself, since he is a rival for her crown, although he seems to be growing a little feeble of wit, to judge by some of his recent letters.'

'But he could be used as a means of obtaining audience with Mary without the rest of the Scottish Parliament becoming aware of it?'

'Probably, although there could be no guarantee.'

'I will settle for the mere possibility,' Cecil said. 'I wish you to take yourself to Edinburgh, or wherever this Arran may be found, and prevail upon his good offices in order to acquire an audience with the Scots Queen. Then you are to advise her privily that Elizabeth wishes to secure the succession to her crown by appointing Mary as her heir, in recognition of which she will be offered the hand in marriage of one of our leading nobles, the newly elevated Earl of Leicester.'

'Dudley?' Randolph asked in mild surprise. 'Is he not the Queen's favourite?'

'And more besides, if the rumour be true,' Cecil nodded, 'but all the more reason why he can be prevailed upon to do Elizabeth's bidding.'

'That should prove no hardship, on this occasion,' Randolph replied. 'They say that Mary of Scotland is beautiful. And, of course, she still enjoys her youth.'

'Yes, yes,' Cecil muttered dismissively, 'but Dudley will do what he is told, for love of Elizabeth and not because of any natural lust for a beautiful lady.'

'Why is this young man present?' Randolph asked with a sideways glance at Tom Ashton, who had been a silent witness to their conversation.

'Because of his unique talents,' Cecil explained. 'Not as a clerk, since his work in that regard is slipshod and grudging. But if there is a lock to be picked, a keyhole to be listened at, or a young maidservant to be seduced for information, then he is invaluable. I wish him to become acquainted with Scotland, since I have a feeling in my waters that we shall be much engaged there in matters of, shall we say, secretive activity in the next few years.'

'You fear that the Scots will prove false, my lord?'

'I have no doubt whatsoever that the arrogant and headstrong Mary will pursue what she regards as her rightful claim to the throne of England, hence the carrot that we are dangling under her nose to become Elizabeth's heir. If you were offered a brand new house, fully furnished and with a household of trusted servants, would you burn it down?'

X

Cecil studied the long dispatch from Francis Walsingham. Walsingham was proving to be a valuable addition to 'Master Secretary's' spy network, but the news he had to impart presaged some careful diplomacy on Cecil's part.

The Queen Dowager Catherine de Medici seemed destined to be Regent of France for the next decade or so, given that the heir, her son Charles, was only ten. In an effort to maintain stability within the realm until he came of age she had urged tolerance towards those Protestants within the country who had become generally known as 'Huguenots', in the same way that Elizabeth in England had been quietly tolerating Catholics. In this Catherine was strongly opposed by the powerful Guise family, one of the daughters of which had supplied France with its recent Queen, Mary of Scotland.

Legislation had allowed Huguenots to worship behind closed doors inside French towns, but openly in country areas and it was in one of the latter, a village called Wassy, in the Champagne region, that Francois, Duke of Guise, contrived to generate an incident that allegedly justified the subsequent massacre, by his armed retainers, of almost the entire Huguenot congregation that had met for worship in a humble barn outside the town wall. The 'Massacre of Wassy', as it became known, had provoked a series of retaliatory armed uprisings led by a self-appointed Huguenot leader Louis of Bourbon, known as the Prince of Condé, resulting in strategic towns such as Angers, Blois, Tours and Lyons falling under Huguenot control.

France seemed destined to descend into civil war, which in one very major sense would be of considerable assistance to England in its desire to keep foreign invaders of any description from its shores, but the Prince of Condé had now approached the English Ambassador Throckmorton for military support from his English Protestant neighbours against the Catholic ruling Valois dynasty. It was clearly in England's interests to lend that support, not only to preserve its public image as a nation that upheld the Protestant form of religion, but also because it provided a convenient, and hopefully a not too expensive, excuse to occupy a key town in Northern France from which the Dutch could be sent military assistance against the occupying Spanish.

Walsingham had made secret arrangements for Condé's envoy Francois de Beauvais to journey across the Channel for urgent negotiations with Elizabeth's representatives and Cecil had sent Robert Dudley back down to Plymouth to arrange for one of Hawkins's vessels to cross the water to Le Havre and collect him. Council had already agreed to send English troops over there in armed conflict, but it might be possible to do so much more cheaply, if Condé held as strong a check over the Valois Regency as Walsingham's dispatch implied. If Cecil got his way, a relatively small force under Thomas Howard could occupy Le Havre, or some other northern French port, on the invitation of the Protestant rebels and then simply decline to hand it back.

This is precisely what happened and Cecil was loudly praised by both Elizabeth and her Council for his negotiation of what became known as the Treaty of Hampton Court, under which three thousand men, largely from the massive retainer force that Howard maintained in the Eastern Counties even in peacetime, took occupation of Le Havre without a blow being struck. But in exchange for additional privileges and a statutory undertaking that there would be no more religious persecutions, the Huguenots agreed to combine with the largely Catholic forces of Queen Dowager Catherine, as Regent of France, to drive the English back out of Le Havre. Howard, seething with impotent rage, was ordered by Elizabeth to withdraw before his entire garrison was slaughtered by superior numbers and the English were again without a foothold across the Channel.

Tom Ashton had already seen enough of Edinburgh to last him a lifetime. The people were dour and unfriendly once they heard their English accents, the food was execrable, the ale was almost undrinkable, and as for the women — well they seemed to Tom to be constructed from the same rancid fat that dripped off every dish that their landlord served up to them.

They had finally received word that they would be received at Holyrood Palace. The two Thomases guided their mounts under the archway of the gatehouse that led to the north west tower of the Palace, in which — or so they had been promised — Queen Mary would receive them.

They handed their horses to a sour-faced stable groom, shook the relentless rain from their riding capes and stepped under the entrance arch, where a liveried menial bowed and scraped them up a staircase and into a lavishly furnished chamber that was the most civilised room Tom had seen since they left London. Heavy tapestries promised protection against the howling gale that was creating music of sorts around the turrets of the upper floors, and a large fire was burning brightly in a generous fireplace, the flames of which cast rippling waves of light upwards and across a large heavy oil painting of some long-forgotten worthy dressed in what looked like animal skins, although there was no mistaking the crown on his narrow head.

The doors at the far end of the chamber opened suddenly and both English emissaries spun round in anticipation of catching their first sight of Scotland's famously beautiful Queen. Instead, out bustled a squat man who seemed to be walking with a stooping forward motion that soon revealed itself as a hunched back. His voice, when he spoke, was certainly not tainted with that awful gargle that seemed to afflict most Edinburgh people, but neither was his English all that easy to follow, since it clearly originated somewhere in mainland Europe.

'My greetings with you, gentlemen,' he lisped unctuously as he bowed. 'You are from the English Queen Elisabetta?'

'Elizabeth, yes,' Randolph confirmed with a frown and the man looked suitably chastened.

'You will be forgiving me, I hope — in my country it is "Elisabetta". I am coming from Italy before I serve my Queen. I am David Rizzio, her Secretary.'

It was Randolph's turn to give a slight bow of acknowledgment as he confirmed his own name and the fact that he had been sent by 'Queen Elizabeth's Master Secretary'.

Rizzio nodded. 'She is wishing to marry her, yes?'

Tom suppressed a giggle as Randolph kicked his ankle in a warning, then corrected what Rizzio had just suggested. 'She wishes to arrange a marriage between your mistress and the finest noble in all England.'

'The name of this man?' Rizzio asked.

'Robert Dudley, Earl of Leicester.'

'We have heard of him. He makes passion with your Queen, does he not?'

'He does not,' Randolph replied loudly and firmly. 'He was once married, but his wife died tragically and now it is to the great advantage of both our nations that he be linked in marriage with your Queen.'

'You have no princes of royal blood to offer?'

'No, but with Leicester comes Elizabeth's undertaking to make your mistress the heir to the English throne.'

'And you have come here today to meet with her?'

'If she would be gracious enough to receive us,' Randolph replied.

Rizzio gestured to two padded chairs to the side of the fireplace. 'If you would seat there, please,' he requested, then hobbled out through the adjoining doors with his unique gait.

They heard the sound of the entrance doors opening once again from the room behind and the swish of a heavy gown on the carpet. They rose and turned and for once in his life Tom was struck dumb.

The first thing that anyone realised when they first cast eyes on Mary Stuart was that she was exceedingly tall for a woman, and indeed would have stood head and shoulders above the average man. Her height was accentuated by her long, graceful neck and high forehead, in which the eyebrows were plucked almost clean, giving her the appearance of one who was perpetually asking a question. The long oval face was flawless of complexion and her deep hazel eyes would have appeared smiling, had it not been for the hooded eyelids that further accentuated the look of enquiry on her face. She was indeed beautiful by anyone's standards, but what stunned Tom into silence was the serenity and confidence with which she gazed out at the world, more than a match for any man or woman. To add to her allure, when she spoke she had a seductive way of pronouncing her words, in an accent that Tom took to be French, given her life history thus far.

She did not hold her hand out to be kissed, but waved her hands in a gentle gesture that beckoned them forward, then stood serenely erect as they came within several feet of her, the look in her eyes somehow conveying the instruction that this was far enough.

'You come from my cousin Elizabeth?' she enquired.

'Indeed, Your Majesty,' Randolph confirmed with a slightly nervous catch in his voice. 'On the instruction of my immediate master, the English Secretary of State, William Cecil.'

'Then who is he?' Mary nodded towards Tom, who wished he could hide under the carpet.

'My clerk only,' Randolph told her. 'Do you wish him to withdraw?'

Tom was hoping that she would agree with this suggestion, but instead she slid her gaze back towards Randolph and assured him that 'That will not be necessary, since my own Secretary is also in attendance.' Only then did Tom realise that the funny little Italian was almost hiding behind her.

'So it seems that I am to be offered the English crown to which I am already entitled only if I marry some English chouchou?'

'Robert Dudley, Earl of Leicester, is nobody's "chouchou", madam,' Randolph replied curtly. 'He is one of the finest, strongest, most manly nobles in the realm.'

'But Elizabeth tires of him anyway, does she not, else she would not be seeking to rid herself of him? Men grow so tiresome when they learn that their best days are behind them and that the lady's fancy has moved on.'

'I know nothing of what you speak, Your Majesty,' Randolph blushed. 'I know simply that my Queen would wish to see the crown of England remain in Tudor hands should she pass into the next world without a natural heir.'

'I am first and foremost a Stuart,' Mary bristled, 'but that does not alter the fact that I am the granddaughter of a Tudor and at least I am not bastard, like your own Queen.'

'I should perhaps advise you that Elizabeth's bastardy was revoked by Parliament some time ago.'

'But not by God,' Mary replied with a smirk. 'In the eyes of the true faith, her mother's lying with her father made her a whore. The throne of England will become mine, as the next legitimate Tudor, whether or not I marry your English *vieux cochon*.'

'Be that as it may, Your Majesty,' Randolph said as he shifted his ground, 'my Queen would wish to see you happily married to a fine English gentleman, thereby ensuring that the Tudor line will continue.'

'She could ensure that for herself, could she not?' Mary countered. 'And if this Leicester person is such a fine match, why does she not take him for her own and let him continue the Tudor line through her womb? Am I being offered soiled goods?'

'Most certainly not, Your Majesty,' Randolph insisted as his facial expression stiffened. 'Am I to tell my mistress that you will not entertain an offer for your hand from the Earl of Leicester?'

Mary smiled somewhat condescendingly. 'At this stage you may tell her that I thank her for her admission that the throne that she currently sits upon is not hers under God's ordinance, but assure her that she may continue to occupy it for her lifetime. As for the offer of her rejected *amant*, I will consider it once I have his portrait and I may see for myself what I am being offered. I can afford to be selective, given the many offers that I have already received, some of them from men who are still, shall we say, unused.'

'I shall happily convey those sentiments, Your Majesty,' Randolph assured her as he bowed.

Tom had been back at his lodgings in Thames Street for barely an hour when Cecil visited him.

'Can't wait to give me more work for inky fingers?' Tom said, then adopted a more respectful tone when he saw the expression on his patron's face.

'I have just had an audience with Randolph,' Cecil told him. 'He tells me that Mary rejected the offer of Dudley's hand.'

'Not quite,' Tom corrected him. 'She seems to think that the English crown is hers by right anyway and graciously allows Elizabeth to wear it — as if she had any choice — but as for the Earl of Leicester, she wishes to know more of him before making any decision. She mentioned the need for a portrait.'

'Does she know that Dudley is Protestant?'

'She did not allude to his religion — only Elizabeth's and that only indirectly, by insulting references to her mother. We certainly said nought to that effect while in her presence.'

'This is good,' Cecil nodded, 'and I shall arrange to have Robert's portrait painted in the most flattering way that money can acquire, then delivered to Edinburgh.'

'I sincerely hope that you will not send me with it,' Tom pouted. 'Edinburgh is the shittiest place I ever laid eyes on and I've seen a few in my time. Why did you send me in the first place?'

'For the very purpose that you are about to fulfil,' Cecil said. 'It will be well known that you accompanied Randolph on his visit to Queen Mary and the purpose of it. You may confidently expect to be approached by messengers sent by others to enquire as to how things transpired and it will be enlightening to see who sends them. Whoever they are, and from wherever their instructions originate, you are to make out that Queen Mary is keen to pursue a match with Robert Dudley. Understood?'

'Of course, but why?'

'Never mind why — just report as I said. You may even soil your hands with a bribe to make your information seem more reliable. And now I must take myself back to Whitehall. I shall expect you in my chambers as usual on the morrow.'

XI

Elizabeth was in her Bedchamber, dressing for a banquet to celebrate the Feast of St Thomas Aquinas. Her dressers fussed around her, while several of her Ladies clustered at the rear of the chamber under the control and guidance of their mother duck, Senior Lady Blanche Parry. First to be draped over Elizabeth's head was her chemise. Out of instinct her hand went to her throat, then she looked down with a frown at the set of keys sitting on her bedside table. Although she was back once again in Whitehall Palace, she doubted that they would be required, but the sight of them reminded her of something important.

'Has Robert arrived yet?' she asked as she turned her head slightly to address Blanche, who shook her head.

'No, my Lady, although since he is biding at Kew, he should be here well before the banquet commences. The weather is dry and the tracks are good for the time of year.'

Elizabeth grunted, both with discontent and at the determined efforts of the tasking matron who was tightening the corset that went over the shift and made every breath a supreme effort. Over that went her petticoat, followed by the farthingale hoop that would cause her topmost gown to billow down over the dance floor later that night. Then at least she got to sit on the side of her bed while the stockings were drawn up to her still dimpled knees, ahead of the rich cloth of gold gown that would set her apart from all the other ladies at Court, who were currently banned from anything that approached an imitation.

Finally, the neck and wrist ruffs were applied separately, ahead of the jewellery that would add to the overall burden and in particular her favourite pearl necklace, a gift from Robert. Then in honour of the occasion a miniature Prayer Book was attached to her girdle and she smiled quietly at the thought of how the Roman scholar whose feast they were celebrating would have reacted to this most Protestant of documents.

It still wanted an hour before they would be required to show themselves in the Banqueting Chamber on the ground floor in order to receive the invited guests, and Elizabeth took a grateful seat in the specially constructed chair that was wide enough to accommodate her ballooning skirts and beckoned her Ladies around her. They included Catherine Carey, Countess of Nottingham and her daughter Lettice Knollys, Viscountess Hereford, in addition to Mary Dudley, Robert's sister and the wife of Sir Henry Sidney. They began whispering among themselves excitedly about the festivities to come and Elizabeth took the opportunity to engage in a hushed conversation with Blanche Parry.

'Go and enquire where Robert has got to. He is the host and the guests will be arriving ere long.'

Blanche scuttled away and the small group of ladies made their way down the private stairs into the rear of the Banqueting Hall, where Elizabeth stood with an angry expression on her face at the continuing absence of Robert Dudley. Blanche scurried over to where Elizabeth was standing, hands on hips and red in the face.

'Well, where is he?' Elizabeth demanded.

Blanche braced herself as she answered, 'He has sent word that he is ill-disposed to attend, my Lady. It would seem that Robert declines to grace our company.'

'Treason!' Elizabeth spat, then lowered her voice as the interest of several Courtiers appeared to be attracted to the sudden outburst. 'Send word to have the Earl of Leicester conveyed to the Tower, on my order!'

'Should we not perhaps first enquire as to the reason for his seeming ill manners, my Lady?' Blanche suggested timorously.

After staring at her in disbelief, Elizabeth nodded. 'Perhaps that were best,' she agreed with obvious reluctance, 'but what of this evening's celebrations? I cannot host them without an escort.'

'I was speaking with the Earl Marshall as you entered with your Ladies and he assured me that he would deem it an honour to be invited to stand in for Robert.'

'Norfolk?' Elizabeth asked petulantly. 'He would no doubt prove to be about as gracious as a wild boar cornered by the pack. But at least he has the rank and title, so let it be. Tell my Lord of Norfolk that he is to sit on my right when I take my place at board.'

An hour later, Elizabeth had suppressed her earlier misgivings and was content to chat away inconsequentially to her conscripted co-host about the state of the counties to the north of the country, for which Thomas Howard was responsible in his capacity as Queen's Lieutenant in the North.

'If I might be allowed to advise Your Majesty outside the confines of your Council Chamber,' Howard oozed, 'it was an inspired decision on your part to offer the hand of Robert Dudley to the Scots Queen.'

'That was Cecil's idea, as you must recall,' Elizabeth corrected him with a hint of annoyance, 'although I must own privily that neither party to the proposed match has shown any great enthusiasm for it.'

'Indeed?' Howard queried. 'I had been led to believe that Mary of Scotland wishes to view his portrait daily in eager anticipation.'

'From whence came that suggestion?' Elizabeth demanded sharply.

'Kitchen talk only, Your Majesty. Actually, a little higher than the kitchen — some lowly clerk that Cecil keeps in his service, who travelled to Edinburgh with Cecil's latest ferret and reported to my man on his return regarding the audience they had with Mary in Edinburgh.'

'And why would Cecil's clerk be reporting to your man?' Elizabeth demanded, somewhat alarmed.

'Perhaps "reporting" was too strong a word, Majesty. It seems that the two have become friendly while dining together in the Common Buttery and it came out in general conversation.'

'Mind me to speak to Cecil regarding the loose tongue of his lowly bred clerk,' Elizabeth replied.

'Until you confided in me just then, Your Majesty, I had assumed that the reason for Leicester's absence this evening, and the occasion of my being honoured with a seat at your side, was that he was preparing to depart for Edinburgh. Or does Your Majesty intend to send him to face those rebellious Irish before he ascends the throne of Scotland? An alliance between Scotland and England would be most welcomed at this time, to defeat the rebellious Irish who have now crossed the sea to promote their outrageous demands in the west of that country.'

'If that heralds a bid on your part to be commissioned to cross to Ireland with an army in my name, then save your breath, my Lord. I have already promised the Viscountess of

Hereford that her husband shall be first considered for that honour.'

'Was that at her request, or his, Your Majesty?' Howard asked with a raised eyebrow.

'It came from her, certainly, but surely she was simply passing on what he had authorised her to request?' Howard inclined his head in an unspoken question and Elizabeth was hooked.

'What means that silence, Norfolk — have I been deceived?'

'Most certainly not, Majesty, in the sense that Lady Knollys without doubt wishes for her husband to be sent to Ireland. But one must ask why a wife would so eagerly seek, for her husband, an honour that might result in his death.'

'She wishes him dead, say you?' Elizabeth persisted, although horrified by what was being suggested.

'Forgive me, Your Majesty — I speak too freely on occasions. But I remain ever mindful of your charge to your new Council, in your very first address to us, at Hatfield, when you commanded that we speak to you privily of any matter that might affect your throne. And rumour has it that Lady Hereford has eyes for a member of that Council.'

'The Privy Councillor of whom Lettice Knollys is said to be enamoured — who is he?'

Howard bowed his head in the manner of one seeking absolution of sin. 'Forgive me, Your Majesty, but even I dare not name him, given that he is so close to Your Majesty's heart.'

'Norfolk,' Elizabeth demanded in a voice rising with panic, 'I command you to tell me who has so engaged the heart of Lady Knollys that she has set about encompassing the death of her husband!'

'I dare not, Your Majesty, in case I am mistaken, or misled by mere rumour. The gentleman in question is too close to the throne and so highly thought of by Your Majesty that he was recently ennobled.'

'Leicester?' Elizabeth all but screamed, then lowered her voice when she remembered the proximity of others. 'You tell me that Robert Dudley is enamoured of Lady Knollys?'

'Forgive me, Your Majesty — I may have been misinformed, or it may be that the lady's affections are not returned, but I spoke only out of an awareness of my loyal duty to your royal person.'

XII

Elizabeth's face was a mask of stern disapproval as the Audience Chamber doors were opened and in walked Robert Dudley with a broad smile. It faded instantly when two guards armed with halberds stepped out from where they had been waiting just inside the door and followed him down the carpet towards where the Queen sat on her throne on a raised platform. She was accompanied only by Blanche Parry, whose face clearly expressed her apprehension.

But Robert was not alone either. A few paces ahead of him walked a servant dressed in the bear and ragged staff livery that Robert and his brother Ambrose had adopted as a symbol of their descent from the Beauchamp Earls of Warwick.

'Finally!' Elizabeth announced loudly and sternly. 'It seems that I have to order your arrest before you grace me with a response to my command that you attend Court. We shall begin, I think, with your explanation for ignoring my original command that you host the banquet to commemorate the Feast of St Thomas Aquinas. Then you might go on to justify — if you can — the five other occasions upon which you ignored my summons to attend Court.'

Robert replied, almost casually, 'I was in Plymouth, Your Majesty.'

'For six weeks?' Elizabeth said petulantly. 'I had messengers wearing the track bare between here and Kew, but all they could glean from your Steward was that you were "absent on the Queen's business". Since I have no recollection of commissioning you with anything other than your attendance here at Whitehall, what manner of business do you claim to have been engaged upon? And why in Plymouth?'

'If Your Majesty would permit,' Robert replied, unconcerned, as he nodded towards the servant a few paces ahead of him. 'Matthew, please open the casket, in order that Her Majesty may view its contents without the need to bend forward.'

Matthew did as instructed and the lid of the casket opened backwards to reveal the fact that inside it was an impressive store of gold coins.

'Ten thousand pounds, Your Majesty,' Robert announced proudly. 'The return on your original speculation of one tenth of that amount in the voyage of Master Hawkins. I was obliged to wait for three weeks in Plymouth while his small fleet was delayed by adverse winds, hence my protracted stay in a poxy inn that I could only recommend for further use as a prison chamber for unwanted visitors to our shores. I had left two days before the banquet, in the belief that Hawkins would be returning three days thereafter, and I was anxious to secure Your Majesty's due from the first sales of sugar, hence my early departure, which in the event proved to be far too early.'

Elizabeth's face had softened from the moment that the casket had been opened and there was almost the hint of a smile as she looked back down the carpet, then gestured with her hand for the guards to step to the side, leaving Robert on his own.

'Does this Master Hawkins intend to make further voyages?' she asked.

Robert nodded. 'He will set sail again next week, Your Majesty, although this time he does not seem to lack those with the necessary finance to act as his sponsors. Perhaps next time, although there is a more general matter that I would seek to raise with you, regarding broader explorations of the oceans. Maybe in more intimate company?'

Elizabeth nodded, waved the guards out of the chamber, called for the pages at the door to bring wine and wafers, dismissed Blanche Parry from her presence and gestured Robert into the seat thereby vacated. Robert dismissed his servant, then walked onto the dais, stooped, leaned forward and kissed Elizabeth's hand.

'I've missed you, my love,' he murmured.

'That's not all you've missed,' Elizabeth replied tartly. 'Thanks to your inaction regarding the advantageous marriage I arranged for you, the Scots Queen has now married another English noble.'

'I had already heard,' Robert nodded. 'Some empty vessel from the northern realm. "Lord Darnley", if I remember correctly. What did he have to recommend him, pray?'

'You mean other than the fact that he was willing to marry her?' came the sarcastic reply that he deserved. 'For all the interest you showed, she might have been the daughter of a fishmonger.'

'Have I not always assured you that there is only one woman I would marry?' Robert responded as he reached for her hand, only to see it hastily withdrawn into her lap.

'So you have no interest in any other woman?' Elizabeth asked innocently.

Robert shook his head. 'No-one other than your beautiful self, as I have sought to assure you all these years.'

Elizabeth blushed, but was clearly not fully convinced. 'During your unexplained absence, I was advised that one of my Ladies had conceived a passion for you,' she pouted.

Robert smirked. 'I cannot be held responsible if another lady finds me more pleasing a prospect than you do, Lillibet. Perhaps you should accept my hand while it is still unengaged.'

'Do not refer to your Queen by the name she was given by her first nursemaid,' Elizabeth rebuked him. 'And how may I be reassured that you have not returned the interest shown in you by Lettice Knollys?'

A look of alarm flitted across Robert's face, to be hastily replaced by one of outrage. 'Who has been filling your ears with such falsehood, pray?'

'The man who replaced you as host at the banquet of St Thomas Aquinas, who has ever served me well.'

'Norfolk?' Robert demanded with a look of disdain. 'He also serves *himself* well, if my information be correct. This piece of wet cloth who has married the Scots Queen is a northern noble, is he not? How can you be sure that it was not Norfolk who brought that about? He has ever sought to oppose my interests.'

'You opposed your own interests, in not marrying Mary when you had the opportunity,' Elizabeth reminded him. 'As for Lord Darnley, he is higher born than you by many leagues, since his mother is my cousin the Countess of Lennox. Should he and Mary have progeny, they will have a claim on both crowns and you did not serve me well by spurning her hand.'

'Even if I did it for love of you?' Robert asked as he reached out for a hand that remained firmly in Elizabeth's lap.

'If you truly love me, pray tell me more of how the fortunes of State may be enriched by your sailor friend Hawkins,' Elizabeth insisted. 'This is what you wished to discuss privily, was it not, and not your empty promises of love and devotion?'

'They are not empty!' Robert protested. 'You did me wrong to tempt me with small favours in our youth, and more recently, only to deny me your hand in marriage while I live a chaste life in your perpetual service.'

'Enough, Robert!' Elizabeth insisted. 'Tell me more of Hawkins and his ventures.'

'It is more his cousin, a man named Francis Drake,' Robert explained. 'I believe I may already have made mention of him and his ambitions to sail around the entire globe. He is convinced that by sailing west, beyond the Americas, he may continue to discover new lands that may yield their riches to England, thereby stealing a match on those arrogant Spaniards who believe that they rule the ocean. But he requires finance and would be greatly reassured and honoured if Your Majesty would be the first to donate to his cause. By this means, of course, any glory and prestige that he may enjoy will also be that of England and its beautiful Queen.'

'Enough of the false and empty flattery, Robert. I would meet this man Drake when he has returned from his latest venture with Hawkins. Do you seek him out on his return and bring him to me. In the meantime, you are to remain here at Court until I say otherwise. And I shall ensure that Lady Knollys is not afforded any further opportunity to gaze upon what could, were it not for your stupidity, have become the King of Scotland. At least the man who now occupies that role can create no problems for England.'

However, the man in question was posing considerable problems for Mary as she sought to grapple with the issues arising from the growing Protestant clamour inside the nation of which she had made her handsome but dissolute husband the joint ruler. His only comfort to her, for a brief while anyway, was in the royal bed, which he lost no time in dominating with his seemingly endless sexual demands, even when it was confirmed that Mary was pregnant with their first child. When they disagreed on whether or not congress between them should continue, Darnley's reaction was to strike her hard across the face and storm out on a drinking spree that lasted the best part of a week.

When Darnley's outrageous behaviour became the talk of the Palace, Mary turned for advice to her trusted Private Secretary David Rizzio, on whom she became more dependent after the birth of her son James. Convinced that his wife was seeking sexual satisfaction with the hunch-backed little Italian, Darnley overpowered the guard to the chamber in which Mary and Rizzio were taking supper, dragging Rizzio out into the corridor, and stabbing him to death.

The murder of Rizzio at the hand of Darnley made him the most hated man in the entire country, even among ardent Catholics, who resented and deplored his treatment of their Queen. Mary came to rely more and more on the guidance and support of one of her leading Catholic nobles, James Hepburn, Earl of Bothwell.

Darnley was ill with smallpox and resting on medical orders in his house at Kirk O'Field when the house was blown apart by gunpowder barrels installed under his bedchamber. His body was later discovered in the garden, in circumstances that suggested that he had been strangled when he sought to escape from the wreckage. While few mourned his passing, such an outrage could not be allowed to go unpunished, and suspicion fell on Bothwell, not least because of his close association with Mary.

Mary was taken by Bothwell to his Borders castle at Dunbar, where she rewarded him with the titles of Duke of Orkney and Marquess of Fife, and a further three days after that they were married in accordance with Protestant rites that did nothing to calm the ire of even Mary's Protestant subjects. Within a month the Scottish Parliament signed a petition demanding Mary's abdication in favour of her infant son James, and when she defied them and prepared for battle at Carberry Hill, on the eastern outskirts of Edinburgh, Bothwell fled the battlefield and eventually died in a Danish prison.

Mary herself was taken prisoner by the rebel Protestant lords and consigned to a gloomy damp existence in an island prison in Loch Leven, near Kinross.

News of all these momentous events was conveyed south to Cecil by Thomas Randolph, who had been sent back north, at Elizabeth's request, following the marriage of Mary to Darnley. Cecil soon came to realise, to his horror, that Elizabeth was reluctant to chide Mary, or to make any overt gesture of support for Mary's Protestant enemies in Scotland, because of any precedent it might set for one monarch to consort in the downfall of another. For all the assurance he had striven to give Elizabeth, and for all his hard work in securing her grip on the crown, his Queen seemed to be haunted by the events of her formative years, in which she had been tossed first one way and then another, by her vengeful and resentful older sister.

Cecil's full attention was demanded when news reached the English Court that Mary Stuart, as she was now generally known, had escaped her island prison and made a final stand against her Scottish opponents at Langside, south of Glasgow. Following a humiliating second defeat, Mary fled south to Carlisle, where she threw herself on the mercy of her English cousin Elizabeth, who immediately summoned Cecil to her side.

'What am I to do, Cecil?' Elizabeth asked, in the same tone of naive desperation that she had employed on that first day at Hatfield. However, her wily old Secretary of State had seen the change in her during the intervening decade and the almost vicious mood swings of which she was capable if thwarted, and he trod carefully.

'The woman is a threat to your throne, Your Majesty, and some might say a disgrace to royalty.'

'Explain yourself, Cecil,' Elizabeth replied with irritation in her voice. 'She is accused of wicked deeds, for certain, but how do we know that those accusations are true? I myself, to judge by alehouse rudery, go to it with every noble at Court and yet I am innocent of such behaviour. And how can she threaten my throne when she is secure inside the walls of Carlisle Castle?'

Cecil sighed inwardly and resigned himself to explaining matters as if to a small child, while maintaining an air of respectful deference. 'As to the latter, she is a Catholic princess of the Tudor line and as such could act as a rallying point for those who cannot accept the changes in our religious observances. As long as she remains alive, there will be those who would seek to engage her in plots against your throne.'

'We should put her to death, say you?' Elizabeth demanded, horrified.

Cecil shook his head. 'Not at this stage anyway, Majesty. She has as yet demonstrated no desire to challenge your right to sit on the throne of England and indeed it is to be hers after your demise, is it not? Forgive me for raising the issue, Your Majesty, but Mary is ten years your junior and even should Your Majesty lead the long and healthy life for which we all pray daily —'

'Dispense with the mealy-mouthed nonsense, Cecil, since your point is well made. But my offer to bequeath her the crown of England was on condition that she marry Robert Dudley. Not only did she not do that, but she married some dissolute oaf who was himself a disgrace to the royal lines from which he was descended, and one has to question whether his son — the young Prince James — is fit to rule England when his turn comes.'

'Which brings us conveniently to my second point, Your Majesty,' Cecil deftly persisted. 'By her actions, Mary Stuart has dragged the image of royalty through the dirt. She married a wastrel, she had him murdered, then she married his murderer, with whom, rumour has it, she had already been engaging in adulterous carnal behaviour. This is hardly the public face that one would wish a scion of the Tudor line to display. Again forgive me, but might not her scandalous actions in some way reflect on the character of her English cousin?'

'Have a care, Cecil,' Elizabeth muttered threateningly. 'Out of respect for your good offices I will assume that you meant to give me wise counsel, but do you mean to imply that I might be deemed capable of such deplorable actions?'

'Far from it, Majesty, since I know you so well. But as you have had cause to learn to your considerable distress, there are those who would seek any opportunity to spread scandalous rumours abroad regarding your own private life.'

'I do not have a private life, Cecil. But that does not, of course, prevent those ill disposed towards me from inventing one for me. And so I ask you this — should we take all these vile slanders against my royal cousin at their face value and therefore assume that they are true, or should we investigate them first, before condemning the woman without any opportunity to examine the facts? That has been my fate and I would not wish it upon anyone else, particularly not a fellow Tudor.'

'You wish me to investigate the allegations against her, Your Majesty?' Cecil asked as his heart sank.

'I most certainly do,' Elizabeth insisted, 'and what is more I will defer any decision on what is to be done with her until you have.'

'As you command, Your Majesty,' Cecil agreed with a bow that was as sweeping as his ageing back permitted.

XIII

'According to that marker stone we just passed, we're almost in Scotland,' Tom Ashton grumbled. Cecil, leading the small procession, appeared not to have heard, so Tom raised his voice. 'Is this some sort of punishment for my slack record copying?'

Cecil reined in his mount and waited until Tom drew level with him.

'Is there no end to your complaining?' the older man protested. 'You could have stayed in London, had you wished, since I had no more desire for your company this past week than you had for mine. But we are both servants of the Queen and we go where we are sent.'

Tom looked up at the forbidding walls of the ancient fortress. 'We must have displeased her mightily for her to send us to this miserable outpost, with dank moorland as far as the eye can see and nothing but the screeching of the marsh birds to welcome us. Where in God's name are we?'

'Carlisle,' Cecil told him.

'You have not even seen fit to explain our "mission", as you call it. Although unless I misheard you, you claimed that it was mine alone. If so, why are you here with me?'

'Because we each have a different mission,' Cecil explained with a sigh of resignation. 'Mine is to enquire of the former Scottish Queen, who is Elizabeth's uninvited guest in yon castle, why she has ventured across the border of her former realm and what she seeks from the Queen of England.'

'And mine?' Tom asked, almost past caring anyway.

'Yours is to continue with what you are best at — seducing female servants. Mary's, on this occasion.'

'Since I do not imagine that Her Majesty has allocated me this pleasurable duty of her own inclination — and indeed I would be surprised to learn that she even knows of it — what is it that you hope I may be able to discover?'

'I will reveal that once we are comfortably installed in the castle yonder,' Cecil replied as he turned his horse's bridle, pointing its head back along the moorland track they had been following. 'You may elect to remain here if you wish, for the carrion birds of whose clamour you were complaining earlier to make a supper of you. Or you may accompany me, in the ongoing pretence that you are my clerk.' He kicked his horse's flank and it continued up the slope with Tom closely behind, still muttering darkly.

Two hours later they had been allocated adjacent chambers in the Captain's Tower that doubled as a gatehouse and was the most comfortable that the Governor, Lord Scrope, could offer to his important, but totally unexpected, guests. When Cecil had advised him of the nature of his business, the Governor had shaken his head sadly.

'The woman seems to have lost all sense of her true predicament. She first came here some weeks ago, heading a sad procession of those who had escaped annihilation further north at the hands of those who now rule Scotland in the name of its young prince. Since then she has been joined by a few servants who drifted in as if driven by the north wind and has set up some sort of royal apartment in the Warden's Tower where I first granted her sanctuary. Now she treats me like some sort of Royal Chamberlain, seemingly unaware that I could drag her out and hang her from the battlements as a foreign invader. I have clearly declined to do so until I am advised of what our own Queen wishes done with her.'

'You were very wise,' Cecil confirmed, 'since even I do not know what is to be done with her. Queen Elizabeth has sent me to speak with her regarding her intentions now that she no longer rules Scotland. But, if I might counsel you privily, never lose sight of the fact that your prisoner is a Tudor and a royal cousin.'

'So what will you say to her?' Tom asked, once they were alone and had been served a hearty supper at a board in front of a blazing fire. Cecil shrugged.

'At this stage, I have not the remotest idea. But are you not eager to learn of your mission? Or is your eagerness confined to the matter of lifting skirts?'

'That and earning riches,' Tom said. 'But I believe that you wish me to lay siege to some Scottish Queen's Lady, else you would not have dragged me here. It may cost you more than fifty pounds this time, since while in Edinburgh I learned that even high born ladies from that country have as much hair on their legs as their fathers and brothers.'

'The size of the fee that you may earn will have more to do with the quality of the information you thereby glean than the comeliness of the lady you bed in order to obtain it,' Cecil said tauntingly. 'But first you must become acquainted with what it is the Queen wishes to know, which I can assure you has nothing to do with how hairy a furrow you are required to plough.' Tom allowed himself a hollow laugh.

'Your turn of speech has coarsened considerably during our renewed association, Master Cecil. But since this fine food and warm fire have inclined me towards sleep, you had best proceed with your instruction.' Cecil's brow creased as he began.

'You are to discover the precise circumstances in which Queen Mary — as she then was — lost her first husband. Not through any carelessness on her part, but when he was killed in an explosion that blew apart the house to which he was then confined, recovering from the smallpox.'

'Have you not answered your own question?' Tom asked as he threw a heavily gnawed pheasant bone into the fireplace.

Cecil shook his head. 'If this man — Lord Darnley — had been killed in the blast, there would have been far more marks on his corpse to confirm that fact. In truth, the only signs of the cause of his death that have been reported lay around his throat, suggesting that he had been strangled.'

'By whom, do we know?'

'The "whom" is not the vital issue. What we — which means "you" — are here to discover is who gave the order for his death.'

'You suspect the Queen Mary?'

'So it is rumoured, which is why our own Queen is reluctant to grant Mary Stuart safe sanctuary here in England. She cannot be seen to condone such wickedness. But there is something else of which you must be made aware. The man she may have commissioned with that dreadful act is the man she then married with indecent haste, in circumstances that raise the gravest suspicions. This second husband was a man called "Bothwell" and shortly after Darnley's death he carried Mary off to his fortress in the borders and there got her with child. Some claim it was an act of criminal violation, but there are others who will assert that they were already lovers, even before Darnley's death. Mary's impregnation by Bothwell is not in dispute, but there remains the lingering doubt as to whether it was by force or by design.'

'And you believe that servants may exist who can reveal the truth of all these well concealed facts?' Tom challenged him.

Cecil nodded. 'Mary Stuart is known to have only a small group of Ladies who attend upon her, at least two of whom are with her here in Carlisle. They are privy to a great deal of intimate information regarding Mary's movements, her innermost thoughts and the doings in her bedchamber. One of these may be persuaded to share some of that knowledge.'

'So I may be required to plough more than one furrow?' Tom said.

Cecil grimaced. 'I leave those matters to you. But Elizabeth must be counselled regarding the true character of the woman who will no doubt seek her assistance to regain her throne. But now it grows late and you are not the only one in need of sleep. I am becoming an old man in the Queen's service.'

'When does my cousin intend to send her army to assist me?' Mary Stuart demanded immediately upon Cecil's entry being announced and before he could even exchange pleasantries with her. 'Or are you merely the vanguard? The Captain in Chief or something?'

'I am no warrior, madam,' Cecil frowned at her hectoring manner, 'nor does Queen Elizabeth at this time have any plans to send troops to your aid.'

'Then why are you here and who exactly are you?'

'Her Majesty's Secretary of State,' Cecil replied with a stiff bow that was almost an act of sarcasm, 'and as such I believe I might be entitled to a seat.'

Mary waved him into a chair adjacent to the one she had vacated when she rose to meet him and Cecil smiled his acknowledgment as he sat down, in the confident expectation that he would not need to engage in any introductory pleasantries.

'Presumably my cousin will agree to assist me in the restoration of my rightful crown?' Mary demanded in a tone that implied that the question was already answered and Cecil took a deep breath before replying.

'Nothing has yet been determined, my Lady.'

'Your Majesty,' Mary insisted haughtily.

Cecil bristled. 'I give that honourable title to only one lady in England, which is where we are currently sitting, so you will perhaps forgive me if I address you as "my Lady". And indeed, as I understand it, even were we a few leagues north, in your native Scotland, it would still not be appropriate to address you as "Your Majesty". Is that not the reality of your current predicament?'

'You are cruel to remind me of it,' Mary scowled, 'but if it will ease our negotiations, we may observe the realities.'

'I am not sent to negotiate,' Cecil told her.

'Then why are you here?'

'To assess your situation and in due course to advise Her Majesty on how best to accommodate you.'

'I am hardly well accommodated in this draughty barn that in my country would barely be appropriate to house cattle,' Mary snorted. 'When may I transfer to London and will you be my escort?'

'Both of those questions were best put to Queen Elizabeth,' Cecil told her and noted the rapid throbbing at her throat as she fought to control her anger.

'And in the meantime?' she demanded and Cecil spread his arms in a gesture of uncertainty.

'Until the Queen issues further orders, you must remain here, it would seem.'

'I would be better to cross the border back into my own country, where I still have loyal subjects,' Mary insisted. 'And, I might add, where I am treated with more deference that you have so far displayed.'

Cecil felt his anger and distaste rising rapidly and it was his turn to fight with his natural instincts. At least he had one way of putting this arrogant harpy in her place.

'I do not believe that journeying north is an option that is currently available to you, my Lady.'

'Because of the perceived danger from the traitors across the border?'

'No, because of my instructions from my Queen that you are to remain where you are until she has decided how best to deal with you.'

'I am a prisoner, say you? The innocent captive of my own cousin?'

'Let us say simply that you are not free to leave here, either to the north or to the south,' Cecil replied with considerable satisfaction.

Mary's face grew instantly crimson, then she rose quickly, turned her back on him and yelled 'Get out, you insolent little servant! And take your impudence with you!'

Cecil bowed gratefully from her presence without another word. There were plenty that he might have employed, but none of them would have assisted in moving matters forward.

Back in the living chamber that he shared with Tom he hurled his bonnet into a corner of the room before realising that Tom was seated in that corner, where he was narrowly missed by the flying headgear.

Tom grinned. 'How went your audience with the former Queen of Scotland? Did she instruct you to piss in your bonnet before hurling it into a corner?'

'She might as well have done,' Cecil grumbled. 'She is quite the most arrogant, high and mighty, unpleasant and overbearing old sow that I ever had the misfortune to encounter and she makes our own Elizabeth seem like a sainted martyr by comparison.'

'So no love lost between you?' Tom smirked. 'Can we therefore plan our departure for tomorrow?'

'Would that we could. But may I take it from that remark that you have not yet identified any pathetic wench in Mary's service that you can tup for information?'

'I have encountered but one,' Tom said, 'and a most comely one at that. Her name is Janet Spittell, but she seems a little high-born for my normal strategy and will require much careful handling, in the manner of a finely bred stallion or mare.'

'But what can she tell us, even should she succumb to your charms?'

'She is the gentlewoman who attends on one of Mary's own Ladies and may therefore have been privy to what obtained in Edinburgh at the date of the death of Lord Darnley and thereafter. She has been in that service for the past two years or so. But I must caution you that she will be a hard quarry to bring down.'

'Do they not say that all the excitement is in the chase?' Cecil reminded him. 'So what strategy do you propose to employ?'

'I must first gain her friendship and confidence,' Tom told him. 'She once fled all her home comforts, rather than marry her father's choice of husband for her, so she is clearly of an independent spirit. She also gives the impression of having once received an expensive education and she is gifted with the skills of an apothecary. No simple country wench, clearly, but I have no doubt that under her skirts she functions much the same as any other woman. But in short answer to your question, I have arranged to walk with her this evening along the battlements of this ancient heap and shall continue to do so until I have either the information you seek, or the pleasure of opening her legs to new experiences. I shall obviously keep you well informed regarding the former, but not the latter.'

'Neither will be possible,' Cecil frowned, 'since I must lose no time in returning to the Queen and advising her of the threat that Mary poses, both to herself and anyone unwise enough to champion her cause.'

'But I have barely begun my assault on Janet Spittell's virtue!' Tom protested.

'I do not recall advising you that you would be riding alongside me when I return to London. And before you protest at my leaving you here to fend for yourself, remember that your mission is as important as mine, if perhaps a little more pleasurable.'

'Will you not find it tedious to travel alone for another week?'

'Not as tedious as the week I spent on the northward journey, with a whining ungrateful clerk for company. See to the conquest of Janet Spittell's affections and ought else that falls into your grubby hands.'

XIV

'God be praised that you got back safely!' Elizabeth exclaimed as she rose from her throne in the Audience Chamber at Whitehall Palace, stepped down from the dais and grasped both of Cecil's hands warmly.

Cecil, for his part, merely smiled. 'If you are referring to the uprising in the north of your kingdom, Your Majesty, I heard tell of it at an inn near Peterborough on my way south, but I saw nothing of it on my travels. It was as if it exploded behind me wherever I rode. How bad is it, pray?' Elizabeth grimaced as she recounted what had been relayed to her by messengers sent south by fast horse.

'It seems that Neville of Westmorland and Percy of Northumberland assembled a large host at Raby Castle and then marched on Durham, which they have occupied in the name of Mary Stuart. They are putting word abroad that all true Catholics are to come to their banners and march on London, there to install Mary as rightful Queen of England. What did you learn of her true intentions?'

Cecil looked uncertain as he told her, 'She is without doubt one of the most arrogant women I have ever had the misfortune to encounter. There can also be little doubt that she sees herself as the next lawful monarch of England. But as for bringing the date of her coronation forward by deposing yourself, I doubt it. Her concern would, at this stage, seem to be to regain her Scottish crown and for that she is all but demanding Your Majesty's assistance. I would be surprised to learn that she is behind this latest uprising, although she is obviously its cause; in that regard she remains a serious threat to Your Majesty, and I would urgently counsel that you have her put to death for her crimes.'

Elizabeth's face lost its eagerness as she shook her head slowly. 'I cannot conceive of doing that until I know of what she is guilty. What did you learn of her possible part in the murder of her husband Darnley?'

'Nothing as yet, Majesty, but I have left Master Ashton behind and he has already engaged the interest of a gentlewoman in the service of one of Mary's Ladies, so in due course I would anticipate that we shall know the truth. But in the meantime, what provisions have been made to meet this latest uprising, which may only be the first of many?'

Elizabeth shook her head in an expression of defeat. 'The Duke of Sussex, as President of the Council of the North, has raised such men as he can afford at this stage, but he constantly demands that more be sent north to swell his ranks. The Earl of Lincoln can raise more, but Lord Chancellor Hatton advises that the Treasury does not currently possess the funds with which to pay more than a thousand men at most.'

'Could we not summon Council and obtain consent to the raising of a new tax?' Cecil asked, then regretted it almost immediately as Elizabeth snorted a reply.

'Half the Council are committed Catholics themselves, Cecil, as you are well aware and for all we know some of them are behind this plot. Added to which we have not summoned them for some time and if we do so solely in order to tax the nation, there will be a popular outcry, particularly from London merchants for whom the north of England is a foreign land.'

Cecil nodded his agreement with a sad face, just as the doors to the Chamber were thrown open by a page.

'The Earl of Leicester and two attendants, Your Majesty.'

Their eyes switched to the end of the Audience Chamber as Robert Dudley walked confidently towards them accompanied by two ruddy-faced men dressed like city merchants, clearly somewhat overawed by their surroundings and apprehensive of their first audience with their Queen. Robert bowed formally and kissed the proffered royal hand before straightening up and waving in the direction of his companions.

'Allow me to introduce Captains John Hawkins and Francis Drake, Your Majesty.'

Each of the men bowed and Elizabeth lowered her head in a gesture of welcome, then turned her attention to Robert.

'I assume that you journeyed to Plymouth in order to bring these men to me? Would that explain why you have been missing for over a week and have you heard of the uprising in the north?'

'Indeed I have, Your Majesty, and my companions are here to offer vessels to transport your troops north to Hull, or wherever else they might best be disembarked.'

'They are most loyal and generous, Robert, but unless you have men at your disposal then there will be no-one to transport.'

'What Her Majesty means,' Cecil explained, 'is that without the finances that we undoubtedly do not hold within the Treasury, we cannot put men into the field. That remains a matter of the utmost secrecy,' he added for the benefit of their visitors. It fell silent for a moment, then one of them cleared his throat and spoke out.

'Might we be permitted the honour of contributing to the Exchequer in this hour of need, Your Majesty?'

'That is most generous of you, Master...?'

'Drake, Your Majesty,' was the reply. 'Francis Drake of Devon and ever your loyal subject.'

Elizabeth's face muscles tightened under her ceruse mask. 'Presumably the same Master Drake of whom I am constantly bombarded with complaints from the Spanish Ambassador?'

'Your Majesty?'

'Piracy on the high seas, according to the Ambassador. His last reported outrage is that you sank several Spanish cargo vessels off the coast of some unpronounceable place across the ocean.'

'That would be San Juan de Ulúa, off the coast of Mexico, Your Majesty,' Drake replied with a slow grin.

'Regardless of the location, Master Drake, what have you to say of the allegation?'

'That it is true, Your Majesty, in the sense that we were able to sink several Spanish "man of war" vessels that attacked us as we were seeking to trade legitimately with the Mexicans.'

'They attacked you, say you?'

'Indeed, as my cousin John Hawkins here can also attest, Your Majesty. We were called upon to defend ourselves after they sank four of our vessels for no obvious cause other than their outrageous claim that the ocean belongs to Spain.'

'But you sank some of theirs?'

'Three, Your Majesty. We were, however, fortunate, in that before their cargoes sank to the bottom we were able to rescue them and bring them back with us.'

'According to the Ambassador, they took the form of gold intended for payment to Spanish traders in order that they might establish trade with the Mexicans.'

'Indeed, Your Majesty. Valued at some thirty thousand pounds in all.'

'And you brought it back to Plymouth?'

'Indeed we did.'

Elizabeth tried to hide the smile and forced a frown onto her face. 'Regardless of the circumstances and even after making allowance for the fact that you were obliged to defend yourselves, Master Drake, what you did constituted an act of piracy. The Ambassador will demand that I punish you, or hand you over to Spain. I would much prefer the former.'

'Perhaps a heavy fine, Your Majesty?' Drake suggested. 'Shall we say thirty thousand pounds, payable to the Exchequer once I can arrange for an armed escort back to London?'

This time Elizabeth couldn't hold back the smile, adding a mischievous chuckle for good measure. 'I can see that we shall become good friends, Master Drake. Cecil, will you instruct the Chamberlain to prepare suitable temporary chambers for Masters Drake and Hawkins here at Whitehall? That way they will be free to join us for supper, along with yourself and Robert. And would you please send word to the Earl of Lincoln and the Duke of Sussex to begin recruiting men to England's cause? We shall nip this rebellion in the bud.'

When Cecil brought the glad tidings to Elizabeth that the uprising was at an end, although its ringleaders had escaped, he was not smiling as enthusiastically as she might have expected and she looked carefully into his eyes.

'There is something else, is there not? Something that will not please me?'

'There is indeed, Your Majesty. It is with considerable regret, although no great surprise, that I have to advise you that I have grounds for suspecting that the man who was behind the entire business is a trusted member of your own Council.'

'I hope for his sake you are wrong, whoever he is, for he will pay with his head,' Elizabeth muttered darkly. 'Whom do you suspect?'

'The Duke of Norfolk, Your Majesty. If you would permit me, I will lay out my grounds for suspecting him and you may then have his neck laid out on the block.'

XV

'I want to see the Queen immediately!' Tom Ashton announced as he appeared in Cecil's chamber doorway before anyone could prevent him progressing through the outer chamber in which he normally worked as a copying clerk.

'I doubt whether she'd want to see you, in that state,' Cecil said as he looked over his desk at the mud that spattered both Tom's hose and his boots and what looked like indelible sweat stains under the armpits of his tunic. 'But to judge by your demeanour and your unexpected return from Carlisle, you have something of moment to impart, so if you unburden yourself to me, I'll seek an early audience.'

'You misunderstand,' Tom insisted. 'This time I need to take my reward in the form of an estate somewhere and only Her Majesty can grant me one. Believe me, I have my reason.'

'So do most men of modest means,' Cecil replied calmly. 'But since you already have an estate that you manage as if it were a piggery, why do you need another one?'

'In order to marry the fine lady I've met, whose father would not approve of me otherwise.'

'I doubt if any father would approve of a man like you as a husband for his daughter, fine estate or no fine estate,' Cecil said. 'But do I deduce that you have finally met someone whose legs you cannot open outside of marriage?'

'I have never before met one that I wish to marry,' Tom explained. 'Be in no doubt that I am serious and that a fine estate is my price for disclosing what I have learned regarding the former Queen Mary's involvement in the death of her husband.'

126

'Close the door!' Cecil demanded urgently and when Tom had done so he was instructed to take the seat in front of Cecil's desk and divulge what he had learned.

Tom shook his head. 'If I do that, you will take it to the Queen and earn the reward for yourself. You have no need of further estates and you have riches beyond avarice. I, for my part, have nothing.'

'Not even your continued life, if you do not reveal what it is you have learned without further delay,' Cecil reminded him ominously. 'One word from me, linking you with a plot against the crown and your head would be feeding the crows on London Bridge. On the other hand, when I am able to pass your information on to Her Majesty, I will be well positioned to argue your cause, always assuming that she is sufficiently grateful for your efforts. I am to take supper with her this evening, to divulge what I have learned regarding the identity of the man whose treasonous ambition lay behind the recent uprising in the north. I can easily add what additional intelligence you have gleaned. Now lose no more time — what may I tell Her Majesty?'

Elizabeth looked far from happy as she sat at the supper table and instructed the page to grant admission to Master Secretary Cecil. She had anticipated the meal with one of her favourite sugared almonds and had lost yet another tooth in the process. It was the third this year and it now lay hidden inside her napkin as Cecil approached the board, bowed and took the seat across from hers that she gestured towards with a languid hand gesture.

'Please feel free to eat, Cecil, before you ruin my appetite with the glum tidings that you foreshadowed during our meeting earlier today. How can you lay the guilt of the recent uprising at the door of my own Earl Marshall and Lieutenant of the North? Surely it fell to his office to suppress that rebellion?'

'Precisely, Your Majesty, and did he?' Why was it necessary to rely upon the President of the Northern Council and the Earl of Lincoln to send the rebels packing? Where was Norfolk?'

Elizabeth tutted with irritation. 'Remember that he is my cousin, Cecil,' she replied with warning in her voice. 'He has many duties here at Court and not merely ceremonial ones. When Robert is away, at Plymouth or so he assures me, my cousin Thomas Howard is required at my side, hosting events at Court. So even though it may be true that others were obliged to take up arms in order to defend my kingdom in the north, you cannot lay the blame for that at Norfolk's door. I assume that there is nothing else?'

'Would that there were not, Majesty, but consider other family connections. Presumably Thomas's sister Jane is also your cousin?'

'Naturally, since they are brother and sister,' Elizabeth replied petulantly. 'What of it?'

'Do you also mind who Jane Howard is married to?'

'Really, Cecil, how can I be expected to follow the personal lives of the entire Howard family? There are so many of them.'

'You may therefore be forgiven for not remembering that Jane Howard is married to Charles Neville, Earl of Westmorland. She took urgent ship to France when her husband retreated with his men into Scotland.'

Elizabeth suddenly looked more solemn. 'So you say that the wife of one of the main conspirators in the recent uprising is Norfolk's sister?'

'Indeed, Your Majesty, and that is by no means the sole Howard connection with treasonous attempts to install the Scottish Mary in your place on the English throne.'

'Go on,' Elizabeth invited him in a far more muted tone than she had adopted a few moments earlier.

'The retreat of Westmorland and Northumberland across the border was not the end of the uprising, Your Majesty, although it may be that this latest pathetic gesture has not been reported to you and in any case is all but suppressed, thanks to Henry Carey, Baron Hunsdon. As the first wave of rebels fell back in the face of the combined forces of Sussex and Lincoln, Leonard Dacre took up a siege position in Greystoke Castle, south of Carlisle, which was not his to occupy anyway, since it rightfully belonged to other members of his family. He also further fortified his own Naworth Castle, which lies nearby and assembled a force of some three thousand men. When Henry Carey challenged him to journey to Carlisle in order to argue his loyalty, Dacre gave battle and having lost he also fled north into Scotland.'

'I am well aware of all this, Cecil,' Elizabeth told him as she stifled a yawn, 'since it was I who authorised Carey to seek an assurance from Dacre that his actions were in defence of my throne and not aimed at assisting the Scots Mary.'

'It is a pity that you did not also instruct him to shake the Dacre family tree, in order to observe what fruit fell from it,' Cecil said.

'More Howards?'

'Indeed, Your Majesty. Leonard Dacre has three nieces, all married to sons of Thomas Howard.'

Elizabeth stared back at him for a moment, then shifted uneasily in her chair. 'The worst that Norfolk can be accused of, it would seem, is his poor choice of relatives. That is hardly treasonous.'

'Your own sister thought that one could be held to account for the treasonous actions of one's cousins,' Cecil reminded her. 'In your case, the Lady Jane Grey.'

'Enough, Cecil!' Elizabeth commanded him with a sour face. 'You do your argument no favour by reminding me of the injustice of those false insinuations.'

'Forgive me if I pursue one aspect of that matter a little further,' Cecil wheedled. 'Your sister Mary demonstrated her position of strength to the whole world by having Jane Grey imprisoned as soon as she was able and there were no more rebellions.'

'Your meaning?' Elizabeth asked with irritation.

'Simply this, Your Majesty — that Norfolk should be committed to the Tower until such time as he can demonstrate his lack of involvement in the northern rebellions. He need not be treated harshly — simply sent to the Tower as a warning to others who might be inclined to challenge your right to rule. Most notably, of course, the Catholic Mary of Scotland, in whose cause the recent rebellions were raised. And I have more news regarding her previous misdeeds that would merit that she be taken out and hanged as a murderess.'

Elizabeth's eyes opened wide. 'Your man has unearthed proof of this?'

'He has, Majesty, although it would seem that it has cost him his heart.'

'How?'

'He was commissioned to lay siege to the emotions of a young lady who serves one of Mary's Ladies and who was well positioned to be aware of the true events surrounding the death of Darnley. However, it would seem that the wily girl turned the tables and ensnared his heart and he is now seeking the gift of an estate from you, in order that they may be wed.'

'Would it not best suit our purpose if they were?'

'Indeed it would, Majesty, but until I learn more of this lady I am inclined to be suspicious of the information that she purports to be able to divulge. It all seems too convenient, to my mind.'

'Be that as it may, what does she say?'

'That on the day that Darnley was killed, Elizabeth was visited in her Palace of Holyrood by the man known as "Bothwell", who was undoubtedly her lover at that time and subsequently became her husband. Shortly after his departure, Mary announced that she had taken it into her mind to attend the wedding celebrations of a Palace servant, something she had never been known to do before. Darnley was at that time laid up in his house in a place called Kirk o' Field, close to the Palace, in which he was recovering from smallpox. It was Mary's habit to visit him every evening after supper and she would have been there on the evening that the house was destroyed by an explosion, had it not been for the visit from Bothwell, which it is believed was by way of a warning, or confirmation that their wicked scheme was about to be executed.'

Elizabeth frowned. 'Be that as it may, Cecil and even if it be true, any crime of which Mary was guilty occurred in her own country, which is not England and we cannot try her in England for a crime — even a heinous one such as murder — that was committed in Edinburgh. I cannot have her put to death for that, and your man must try harder if he wishes to be granted an estate.'

'I told him as much, Your Majesty, and I have no doubt that he will work eagerly in our cause to that end. But what is to be done with the Scots Mary in the meantime?'

'For once I am ahead of you, Cecil. It seems to me that we must keep Mary close confined, but further away from either Carlisle, from which she may still receive assistance from her former followers in Scotland and London, from which others of a Catholic persuasion could easily travel to her side. Also a good distance from the sea and any possible attempt by France, or even Spain, to rescue her. The Earl of Shrewsbury has several large estates in the north of the country, but well south of the border and he has agreed — not that I gave him a great deal of choice — to accept responsibility for the Scots baggage. She will shortly be transferred south to Bolton Castle, where she will be allowed to live temporarily in somewhat straightened, but comfortable, circumstances and we may send your man there in order to discover whether she continues to plot for my throne, while flushing out others who might be sympathetic to her cause.'

'And Norfolk, Your Majesty?'

Elizabeth sat for a moment with a frown, then nodded. 'It shall be as you advise. Imprisonment in the Tower, but under such mild conditions as may be experienced in there. See to it that he is not oppressed in any way — other, of course, than with the loss of his liberty. And the moment that his innocence is established, he is to be released. Is that clearly understood?'

'Yes, Majesty. And now, if I may withdraw, I have much to arrange.'

'Indeed. And see that your man is well watched for any sign that he may have been drawn into Mary's web of intrigue.'

Cecil bowed and withdrew from the Audience Chamber. On his way down the hallway outside, he became aware of the

Spanish Ambassador Guerau de Spes waiting for an audience with Elizabeth. The Ambassador's face was a beetroot red and he appeared to be chewing his own gums in suppressed anger. He and Cecil had never formed the same friendly relationship that Cecil had enjoyed with de Spes's predecessor and Cecil nodded curtly as he passed, then allowed himself a smile as he anticipated the angry exchange that was no doubt about to occur in the Audience Chamber he had just left.

De Spes burst into the Chamber before its doors had been fully opened for him and he made an insolent point of omitting to bow as he approached the board from which Elizabeth was distractedly removing a jellied fruit.

'I am here to express the anger and disappointment of my master King Philip!' he thundered, as Elizabeth's face hardened at the studied insult.

'So overcome with anger that you forget to bow, Senor Ambassador?'

'I do not bow to Spain's enemies!' he insisted.

'And I do not grant audience to men of insolence who cannot even observe the basic courtesies,' Elizabeth responded in a warning tone that de Spes either failed to notice, or chose to ignore. 'Particularly not when, as you can see, I am at supper. In the circumstances, you will forgive me if I do not invite you to join me?'

'You employ pirates to challenge the right of Spain to exclusive passage across the oceans of the world and when my master insists that these thieves be handed over for trial in my country, you refuse to comply!'

'I was not aware that I was answerable to the King of Spain for the legitimate actions of English mariners when their vessels are attacked without just cause,' Elizabeth replied coldly. 'And if you are referring to Captains Drake and

Hawkins, I can advise you — since it would seem that the true facts have been withheld from you — that they were acting solely in their own defence when attacked without lawful justification by Spanish ships.'

'They stole much gold!' de Spes shouted, even redder in the face. 'Gold that should now rightfully be in the hands of my master.'

'As I understand the matter,' Elizabeth replied coolly, keeping the smile from her face, 'that gold would now be on the bottom of the ocean, since it was on board several vessels that my sailors were obliged to sink in order to preserve their own lives and those of their crews.'

'They had no right to be where they were,' de Spes insisted, 'since those waters belong to Spain.'

'I had always assumed that the only king they belong to is Neptune,' Elizabeth jested as the smile finally broke through. 'Has your master recently acquired the use of a trident and learned to breathe underwater?'

'Do not jest in this matter,' de Spes replied angrily, 'since my master claims title to all the seas on which Spanish ships have sailed.'

'And the seas that they have not sailed?' Elizabeth countered, to which de Spes had no answer. Taking advantage of his silence, Elizabeth pressed her point. 'No one monarch can claim to rule the oceans, Ambassador. England insists on its right to plough the seas in the course of legitimate trade with other nations and will not be deterred in this by acts of aggression on the part of your sea captains. You may so advise your master, while adding that should ownership of sea lanes depend upon which nation sails them first, then Spain shall soon learn to its cost that England has the braver navigators and explorers. If there is nothing else, good day to you. And see to it that you bow on future occasions.'

A few minutes later, Elizabeth was joined at the supper table by Blanche Parry, and complaining about the looseness of another tooth, when the arrival of Robert Dudley was announced. Elizabeth rose from the table and hurried to meet him, kissing his cheek and steering him to the table by his arm.

'I've missed you, where have you been? There's so much to tell you, particularly about the woman I almost had you married off to. If you'd done my bidding, she wouldn't be posing such a threat to England now.'

'And I wouldn't be free to take supper with you here at Whitehall, would I?' Robert replied flippantly as he took the seat next to hers. 'As it happened, I dined with Cecil — at his request no less — earlier today and he told me of the mischief that the woman is waging up north. I had of course known of the uprising, since it was what we mostly talked about when I was last here. As for what has kept me from your side since then, I am in the middle of repairing my castle at Kenilworth, which has fallen into grievous ruin in recent years. When it is finally completed, you must visit me and bring the Court with you — it will be splendid enough for that purpose, I warrant.'

'I wish you to return to Plymouth without delay, Robert,' Elizabeth insisted.

'Whatever you wish,' Robert replied breezily. 'Master Hawkins has more keels laid and will soon have a fleet worthy of the name with which to defend our shores.'

'And where is Master Drake?'

'Resting in Plymouth, ahead of his intended voyage around the globe. It seems that he no longer lacks the funds.'

'This is good,' Elizabeth confirmed. 'I wish you to lose no time in advising him that while we can commit no finance to his venture, he goes with my blessing and may fly the English flag from his stern wherever he journeys. In particular he is to take no nonsense from the Spanish. He sails in the name of England and its Queen.'

'What did the Queen say?' Tom asked breathlessly as he followed Cecil towards his inner office, where another man sat waiting for them. Cecil waved his arm in the air for Tom to come inside, then pointed to the remaining seat.

'You will need to work harder for your coveted estate, Tom Ashton, but all is not lost. You are to journey to Bolton Castle, wherever that may prove to be and you are to do so in the company of this man. His name is Francis Walsingham and he is twice as skilled in underhand dealing as you, particularly since he does not go about it by seducing innocent maids. Francis, this is the young rogue I mentioned briefly before attending upon the Queen.'

Tom held out his hand, which Walsingham ignored, although he nodded in recognition of the gesture. Tom looked back at Cecil with raised eyebrows and a pained expression. 'Why must I journey away again, what reason did the Queen give for not granting me my estate now, for the valuable work I have already done, and why am I condemned to work alongside a man who will not even shake my hand?'

'That is something else you must earn, Tom Ashton,' Walsingham replied with a soft but confident voice. 'I know nothing of you other than what Cecil here tells me and it is not good. If you prove to be as devious, treacherous and debauched a man as Cecil has described, then we are destined never to shake hands. If, however, you can employ your depraved talents in my service without covering me in your own shame, then perhaps we might get on well enough.'

'Cecil obvious did not also advise you that I am a changed man,' Tom protested. 'Nor am I a man who takes kindly to being so insulted. I withdraw my offer to shake your hand and will only replace it when I deem it appropriate.'

'This is most amusing,' Cecil smirked, 'but perhaps the pair of you could arrange to bicker like country neighbours at some other time, since I have an important mission for you both.' It fell silent and Cecil continued. 'I've been busy and have already made arrangements for Tom to enter service at Bolton Castle. I seem to recall that he has experience and skill with horses, so he'll be employed as a stable groom and will report anything he learns to Francis, who will then take steps to confirm its veracity.'

'Why will that be necessary?' Tom bristled. 'Do you not trust in what I may be told by Jenny Spittell?'

Cecil nodded towards Walsingham. 'Tell him, Francis.'

Walsingham smiled unpleasantly as he explained, 'It seems to me, and Cecil agrees with me, that you may be the victim of subterfuge yourself, young man. He and I have a wealth of experience in underhand dealings and with all due deference to your past successes with simple young country girls, this latest one sounds too confident by half. She has wormed herself into your confidence with ease, playing you at your own game and may seek to use you, either by passing on information that is false, or by gaining knowledge, through you, of what arrangements Queen Elizabeth has made to spy on the Scots Mary. For that reason I will be lodging in nearby towns, posing as a merchant of some description. When you confide in me what you may be told by this Mistress Spittell, it will be my duty to investigate it further.'

Tom opened his mouth to protest, then realised that he would probably be wasting his time. He'd go along with it until such time as both men who were employing him came to realise that he was not being duped and that the least reward the Queen could give him for his invaluable underhanded work was an estate large enough to impress Jenny's father.

'Now, if you will excuse me, I have a few other urgent matters to attend to, but we shall meet again in here first thing on the morrow,' Cecil told them by way of a polite request for them to leave, which they did. The mutual antipathy between Tom and Walsingham that had already begun to manifest itself was further underlined when, upon leaving Cecil's chambers, they stalked off in different directions.

The following morning, shortly after breakfast, they sat back in the chamber in which they had been introduced the previous afternoon, waiting for the arrival of Cecil and avoiding eye contact. After over half an hour of excruciating silence their discomfort was ended as Cecil busted into the inner chamber, bleary eyed and in urgent need of a barber.

'I have barely slept, so please do nothing to further invoke my ill humour,' he snarled as he threw himself into the chair behind his desk, before extracting a crumpled sheet of vellum from his tunic and handing it to Walsingham. 'These directions will guide you both to Bolton Castle, which you can approach by way of Barnards Castle. You are expected there, and Tom should report to Sir Francis Knollys, whom the Queen has appointed as Mary's custodian, although the castle itself belongs to Baron Scrope. Francis, it would be best were you to avoid abiding in the same inn for more than a few days at a time, since it would ill suit your pose as a merchant. But of course you must let Tom know where you may be found at any given time.'

'I know my duties and how properly to conduct them,' Walsingham growled and Cecil glared at him through red-ringed eyes.

'I do not doubt that, else you would not have been commissioned for a task that has now become all the more urgent.'

'What task?' Walsingham asked.

Cecil seemed to sag as he replied, 'The Pope has excommunicated Elizabeth, which is why I have enjoyed little sleep. I have yet to convey the grim tidings to the Queen herself.'

Walsingham snorted derisively. 'Why should she — or any of us — concern ourselves if that over-fed, self-opinionated and blasphemous monk has taken to waving bell, book and candle in her direction?'

Cecil sighed. 'Clearly, not for that reason alone. But he has also absolved all her subjects from any obedience to her commands and has threatened excommunication to anyone who does obey her. This can only inspire the Catholics of this nation, of which there are still far too many, and it makes the Catholic Mary the obvious icon around whom to unfurl their banners of rebellion. Your mission has suddenly become all the more vital for England.'

XVI

They had been on the road for over a week, with barely a word between them. Walsingham had kept his mount slightly ahead of Tom's, whether in order to more accurately follow the crude map with which Cecil had supplied him, or to avoid conversation with his travelling companion, it was difficult to tell. Not that Tom was in the mood for conversation anyway — he was still brooding deeply over the seeming disregard for the valuable information that Cecil had been able to pass on to the Queen and the fact that he was returning to Jenny's side without a better estate of his own.

Even when they were obliged to break their monotonous journey overnight at some wayside inn or another, Walsingham had seemed disinclined to talk, citing the need for discretion in all their actions and conversations and taking himself off to their shared chamber so early in the evening that Tom had been able to hear his snores well before he opened the chamber door to take his own rest for the night.

However, once they were two days north of Lincoln Walsingham was obliged to say something, given the sickening sights that met their eyes. More than one isolated village appeared to have been consumed by fire, and every country crossroad they came to had retained the rotting and grisly remains of men, women and even children who had clearly been hanged some weeks previously.

'Should you ever have cause to doubt the importance of the mission on which you have been sent,' Walsingham muttered grimly as they held their breath against the stench from the latest collection, hanging in the faint breeze and crawling with flies, 'then cast your mind back to scenes such as this.'

'Who are they?' Tom asked, sick to the stomach.

'It is more a case of who were they,' Walsingham replied with a knowing grimace. 'While I cannot give you their names, I can all but guarantee that they were once Catholics.'

'How can you be so sure?' Tom asked.

Walsingham shrugged. 'Almost everyone this far north is of the old faith, blindly following the heretical preachings of the fat Bishop of Rome. This is why it was so easy for the rebels to recruit men in the cause of the pretender, the Scots Mary. What we are passing almost hourly is Elizabeth's response; while they may not have fought for the treasonous cause personally — and certainly their wives and children would not have done — it doesn't matter to her. They are Catholic, this is Catholic country, and the message must be spread without mercy that support for either Rome or Mary Stuart can only mean death.'

'The Queen is crueller that I had been led to believe by Cecil,' Tom mumbled in horror as he watched the decomposing remains of a young girl slip from an inadequate rope and slither to the ground, where they received immediate attention from a pack of ravening dogs.

'The Queen is fearful for her own life, which is why she displays such cruelty, in the hope that it will discourage others,' Walsingham replied, apparently without any emotion. 'She fears rebellion because she has witnessed so many in her life, particularly during the reign of her late sister Mary, when Elizabeth's own name was often falsely added to the list of conspirators. She now sees intrigue and betrayal at every turn — in every nook and cranny of her palaces, even — and is apprehensive that Mary Stuart will be the rallying beacon for a Catholic uprising aimed at removing her from her throne.'

'I was informed by Cecil that the Queen was tolerant of Catholics,' Tom objected.

Walsingham nodded. 'So she was — once. But they have proved themselves treacherous and now, in her fear, she begins to persecute them just as vigorously as her sister persecuted Protestants like ourselves. I assume, since you still retain your head and since you serve Master Cecil, that you are of the Protestant persuasion?'

'Insofar as I am anything,' Tom replied reluctantly. 'Religion has never been important to me.'

'Hence your Godless ways,' Walsingham reminded him bluntly. 'However, God has a purpose for every one of His children, even the wicked ones such as yourself and once we reach our destination you may resume your licentious ways in England's cause. Just remember that your higher duty is to report to me, without fail and without delay, anything you may learn of Mary's involvement in plots against Elizabeth.'

Late on the afternoon of the tenth day their tired mounts all but limped down the single street through a village called Leyburn and Walsingham consulted his chart as he pulled gently on the reins and looked up at a dust-coated sign that hung outside an equally dusty looking inn.

'Here we are — "The Kestrel". Its landlord is apparently expecting a Flemish merchant called Felix Westerhaus, a gem dealer from Antwerp. You will find me here for the next few days and should I choose to move on so as to give rise to no suspicion as to my true purpose, I will leave word as to where I may be found. Now on you go.'

'Where to?' Tom asked. 'You have the piece of parchment that Cecil entrusted us both with.'

'And I shall retain it, as further evidence of my trade as a travelling dealer,' Walsingham said teasingly. 'But if you continue along this track for a further hour or so, you should then see the turrets of Bolton Castle and if you do not know what to do next, then I was correct in my belief that you are not fit for this work.'

Still stinging from this insult to his ability, Tom dismounted at the stables of Bolton Castle and strode to the front entrance, where he advised a somewhat doubting Steward that Sir Francis Knollys was expecting him. He was kept waiting for a considerable time in a small room to the front of the building, some of the outer walls of which still bore the remains of scorch marks from the days when it had been burned in retaliation for its involvement in the Pilgrimage of Grace and had never since been repaired. From where he was standing Tom could see much coming and going in and out of the south-west tower, which he assumed housed the owner. He heard movement in the doorway and turned to see an elderly man whose facial expression suggested that he was carrying the burdens of the entire world on his shoulders.

'You are Cecil's man?' he enquired.

Tom nodded.

'I am Sir Francis Knollys,' the old man told Tom, 'and my daughter Lettice attends upon the Queen as one of her Ladies. The Queen Elizabeth, of course. As for the other so-called queen who resides in that tower that you were so admiring when I entered, it is my thankless task to keep her secure, but to allow her such modest comfort as she seems to regard herself as entitled to. You are to assume duties in the stables, as I understand the dispatch I received from your master?'

'That is correct,' Tom confirmed. 'Where will I be accommodated?'

Knollys reacted with a frown of disapproval. 'It is easy to see that you are not accustomed to such work. You will reside in the loft above the stables, along with the other grooms. I ask only that you do not damage the horses — perhaps it would be best if you attend only to your own.'

'I have worked as a farrier,' Tom replied stiffly, 'and was brought up around horses. And so I bid you a good day and will proceed to my new quarters, lest anyone should question why the lord of this fine estate is entertaining a mere stable groom in the house.'

'It is not my estate,' Knollys explained. 'It belongs to Lord Scrope and I am, like yourself, merely employed here. In my case, as the jailor of a most difficult and demanding prisoner. But do not let me delay you.'

For the next few days Tom relaxed in the familiar surroundings of a large stables, with its reassuring smells of straw and dung, far removed from intrigues and challenges to the brain that were not really his strong point. He had almost forgotten why he was really there when, shortly after sunrise on his fourth day, he froze to the sound of a familiar voice.

'Tom — is that really you?'

He turned, the rake full of the detritus from the empty stall that he was in the process of cleaning still in his hand and there stood Jenny, her facial expression a mixture of hope and uncertainty. Tom grinned as he propped his rake up against the side of stall, then looked hastily from side to side before striding the half dozen paces to where she stood just inside the stable entrance. As he embraced her and kissed her hotly and passionately on tightened lips, he felt her recoil slightly from him and break off the kiss, then look him up and down with a look of distaste.

'To judge by the smell, your circumstances have hardly improved. I take it that the Queen has not only failed to grant you an estate, but has punished you by employing you in this way?'

Tom led her into the open air, then guided her down the side of a yew hedge, where they would not be visible from the castle. 'Clearly my current employment is but a ruse. True it is that I currently have no estate such as would impress your father, but at least we are back together. Do you still serve the Lady Mary?'

Jenny nodded. 'Her favourite attendant, anyway. Mary Seton, mind I mentioned her? She is currently breakfasting with Queen Mary, and I must return shortly in order to attend to the irons when my mistress dresses Mary's hair. I came down here in order to satisfy a curiosity I formed yesterday, when looking out of a chamber window in our prison and saw you exercising a fine mare in the inner keep.'

'That was a deliberate ploy on my part,' Tom announced proudly, 'and it was clearly successful. I was advised that you were all housed in the south-west tower — it looks better than your lodgings in Carlisle, anyway.'

Jenny took his hand, pulled him towards her, then recoiled from the smell of his clothing. 'Forgive me if I do not embrace you, but be assured that when you smell less like a horse's back end I shall not hesitate to do so. I have missed you and feared that you would not know that we had been transferred from that awful castle in Carlisle. At least here we are better accommodated. Queen Mary is allowed more servants and we are all better fed. But what does Elizabeth intend shall be her fate? If the block or the gallows, then surely she would not treat her so well?'

Tom shook his head. 'The Queen does not consult me in these matters,' he told her, 'but she has — or rather, my master Cecil has — sent me back north for any further information I might glean of Mary's plotting against Elizabeth's crown.'

'And once again I am to be your eyes and ears, even though the last intelligence I gave you did not yield you an estate?'

'If you could undertake to do so, that would of course bring our marriage that much closer,' Tom said. 'But do you not feel guilty, betraying your mistress?'

'Not with marriage to you as the prize. In any case, Mary Stuart is not my mistress, Mary Seton is. As for Mary Stuart, the looks she gives me suggest that I belong somewhere under her shoe, in the same way as that gong from the stables appears to have made a permanent home under your boots.'

'So have you anything to report?' Tom asked eagerly.

Jenny looked down at the ground, as if reluctant to reply. 'You must not be offended or disheartened in any way by what I have to impart, but must keep always in mind that I do what I do in order to speed the happy day when we become man and wife. Anyway, I have learned that Mary Stuart is in secret contact with one of your most important nobles — a man called the Duke of Norfolk. You know him?'

'I know of him,' Tom assured her. 'What do you know of any communication between him and Mary?'

Jenny looked into his eyes questioningly. 'You will not think ill of me?'

'I could never think ill of you,' Tom replied encouragingly. 'So what have you learned?'

'Well, it seems that this Duke of Norfolk is presently in the Tower, but has been allowed certain freedoms, one of which is the maintaining of correspondence with the world beyond his prison walls. He has taken to writing to the Lady Mary, making use of what I have heard described as "ciphers", whatever they might be. I hear loose talk between Mary and my mistress on those occasions when I am instructed to accompany her, so as to make Mary's audience seem all the more grand. She is most vain in that regard. Anyway, there is much talk — well, giggles, really — regarding this Norfolk's request for Mary's hand in marriage in return for placing her on the throne of England. There is a wealthy man from Florence who is to send money for troops to achieve this and it is to happen soon. One of their first actions will be to release Norfolk from the Tower, then I believe that they will seize the Queen's person.'

Tom was stunned. Then he remembered Cecil's caution regarding the reliability of any information passed on by Jenny. Was she inventing all this — perhaps at Mary's instigation — in order to see how Elizabeth reacted? Was it designed to cause the Queen to over-react and look either stupid or vindictive in the eyes of the world? He desperately wanted to believe what he was being told, but it was not for him to decide its truth or otherwise. He would need to speak urgently with Walsingham.

'Why do you grow silent?' Jenny asked.

Tom was obliged to mask his suspicion. 'I was simply wondering how we can be certain that these letters that are being delivered to Mary come from Norfolk.'

Jenny looked crestfallen as she replied, 'That is why I asked a moment ago that you not be offended or disheartened.'

'Why would I be?'

'Well, the messenger who always seems to arrive just before Mary receives news that seems to make her happy and almost like a young girl at a village fair, claims to be Norfolk's senior secretary. His name is William Barker and he boasts openly to me of how he is entrusted with his master's most confidential communications — in the hope, I believe, of becoming better acquainted with me and perhaps engaging my affections. You are not angry with me? Only it seems to me that by playing him along I can learn much of the intrigue that is afoot in there,' she concluded as she jerked her head back towards the south-west tower.

Tom treated her to a broad smile that took every effort on his part to fake. 'Of course not, my sweet, but I must hasten in order to pass on this vital information to someone nearby who can convey it to the Queen without delay.'

He retrieved his horse from the stables and rode hard to Leyburn, where he was just in time to see Walsingham climbing onto his own horse from the mounting block outside The Kestrel. He frowned as Tom cantered up alongside him and repeated every word of what Jenny had told him. Then he nodded sagely.

'This may explain why I am summoned back to London in haste. At least I will have something to report in return for spending three nights in this dreadful whorehouse. Resume your intelligence duties here until instructed otherwise,' he ordered Tom as he kicked his horse's flanks and made off along the southern track towards York.

Elizabeth looked fearful as she sat staring at Cecil and Walsingham, who had not slept for two days and who had been rushed into the presence by Cecil when he passed on what Tom had learned.

'Well, gentlemen,' she said, 'what do you propose that I do? The rumours come from three independent sources and cannot go unheeded.'

'Indeed they cannot,' Cecil confirmed,' and what Walsingham has learned seems to confirm what we have been advised by others.'

Three days previously, Robert Dudley had returned urgently from one of his regular journeys to Plymouth, bearing news from Captain Hawkins. Hawkins was the chosen mariner to convey Spanish Ambassador de Spes from Spain to England and back home again, while engaged in his many duties. Because he paid well, Hawkins always made sure that there was ample reward in the form of food and drink and the Ambassador had grown too fond of the rum that Hawkins regularly brought back from the Indies. In his cups he would reveal far more than was appropriate for an ambassador and from him Hawkins had received a slurred confidence regarding a change of monarch that was being planned for England.

Philip of Spain had apparently acquired the services of an Italian banker called Roberto Ridolfi, who could travel around Europe with large sums of gold and a heavily armed escort without attracting undue notice. He in turn was in regular communication with an English noble who could convert that gold into armed men and lead a rebellion against Elizabeth that would see an end to her rule and the restoration of the true faith in England under Mary Stuart.

While this might otherwise have been discounted as the wild ramblings of an inebriated and self-important little Spanish emissary, what he was confiding had been partly confirmed by an urgent dispatch that Cecil had received, in his capacity as Secretary to the Queen, from the Grand Duke of Tuscany, Cosimo de Medici, who was alarmed at the recent increase in the Spanish presence in Italy and anxious to promote warfare between Philip of Spain and other monarchs of Europe. Cosimo himself was the son of a wealthy banking family, had learned of Ridolfi's intrigue with Spain through mutual associates, and was hopeful that by alerting Elizabeth to the plot against her life and rule he would provoke her into declaring war on Spain. In this he had been unsuccessful, but he had at least sounded enough early warning to prepare her for what was about to occur.

'How sure can we be that my cousin Norfolk is implicated in all this?' Elizabeth asked.

Cecil inclined his head to the side. 'At present it is no better than the tittle tattle of one of Mary Stuart's ladies, Your Majesty, but I have never known Tom Ashton to give me false information.'

'Perhaps you have never sufficiently tested him,' Walsingham replied grumpily, 'but at all events we cannot sit and do nothing.'

'No-one is suggesting that for one moment, Walsingham,' Elizabeth replied testily, before turning to address Cecil. 'How would it suit were we to have Norfolk hung drawn and quartered on Tower Hill? The mob have been starved of entertainment thus far during my reign.'

'I was about to suggest that we release him with an apology,' Cecil said.

Elizabeth's eyebrows shot up in sheer disbelief. 'This is no time for jests, Cecil.'

'I do not jest, Majesty,' Cecil replied calmly. 'As matters stand, he will deny any involvement, should we task him with it, or even have your torturer put him to the question. Far better that he be allowed his freedom and be led to believe that he is trusted. Then we keep him and his servants under close observation until we catch them at it, in circumstances that leave no room for denial. Then and only then, we give him a traitor's farewell.'

'Your man in Mary's camp can be relied upon, I assume?' Elizabeth asked.

'He most certainly can,' Cecil confirmed, 'but I would have someone investigate more closely into the origins of the gentlewoman who supplies him with his information. Perhaps Walsingham here?'

'No,' Elizabeth replied firmly. 'I wish him to travel to Paris without delay and relieve Throckmorton of his duties as our Ambassador to France. Is there no-one else you can send? No one you could trust with such a delicate business?'

Cecil thought for a moment before replying. 'There is my son Robert,' he told her. 'He is currently engaged as my Senior Clerk and there is little of love lost between himself and Tom Ashton, for reasons that date back to their youth, when Tom resided with me during his years of service to you when you were in peril from your sister Mary.'

'Yes, I well remember his excellent service at that time, although I also seem to recall that he is something of a rogue and that Blanche Parry detests even the mention of his name.'

'Indeed, Your Majesty, but he has talents that can be put to good use in England's cause, as they are being now. However, I need to test the veracity of the information he is passing on from one of Mary Stuart's coterie of women, since I have suspicions that this woman is playing him at his own game. I therefore propose to send my son Robert north to where Mary is being held, in order to replace Walsingham as my messenger and also to learn what he can of this woman's origins.'

'Do that, Cecil and with my blessing. As for you, Walsingham, rest here in London for a respectable period, then take yourself off to Paris.'

It proved all too easy. Cecil had barely put the wheels in motion when he was approached, through an intermediary, by a Shrewsbury draper called Thomas Browne, who was actually shaking with apprehension as he explained to Cecil that he had recently been entrusted with a large heavy bag by two of Norfolk's secretaries, William Barker and Robert Higford. He had been asked to deliver it to one of Norfolk's officials in York. He begged Cecil's forgiveness for having opened it and pleaded his innocence of what he had found inside it when curiosity got the better of him, due to its weight, as he stayed overnight at an inn in Gainsborough. There was over six hundred pounds in gold from the French Ambassador, a collection of letters written in a cipher of some sort and instructions to the recipient that the gold was to be smuggled into Mary Stuart's prison apartments with the compliments of the Queen Dowager of France, Catherine de Medici.

Browne was aware that Mary Stuart was currently a prisoner of Her Majesty and that Norfolk himself had only recently been released from the Tower following accusations that he had been behind the uprising in the north that had been visited with such brutal reprisals, and he was terrified that he might somehow have become innocently involved in something treasonous. Cecil assured Browne that his loyal service would be reported to the Queen and he was given a hundred pounds in exchange for his silence.

A man employed by Cecil who was skilled in ciphers was soon able to advise his employer that, so far as he could make out, the money was intended to be used to enable Mary Stuart to bribe appropriate men at Bolton Castle to facilitate her escape when word came that troops had landed in England to overthrow Elizabeth, and that the balance of the money would ensure her a heavily armed escort as she journeyed south to

York to be crowned. Barker and Higford were tortured in the Tower until they revealed that the master key to the cipher was to be found in the Howard House in Temple Bar. It wasn't, but a thorough search by royal men at arms, under strict instruction from Cecil not to cease looking until they found something, eventually yielded a ciphered letter in Mary's own hand, hidden under a doormat. The 'Ridolfi Plot' was at an end.

Confronted with all the evidence against him, Norfolk reluctantly conceded that he had allowed his name to be used in order to persuade Mary to rise up and claim the throne of England, but denied any ambition to marry Mary himself, or any plot against Elizabeth's life. A badly shaken Elizabeth had him tried on three counts of treason, her only concession towards the fact that they were cousins being that when he died on Tower Hill, Norfolk was merely beheaded and not hung, drawn and quartered, the usual penalty for treason.

However, Elizabeth was less inclined to accept that Mary deserved the same. In an angry exchange with Cecil the day after Norfolk's execution, she pointed out that 'She could have been the innocent dupe of others, Cecil. I mind how I was blamed for every attempted uprising against my sister Mary, when in truth I knew nothing other than the fact that they acted in my name, but without my blessing.'

'Even so, Your Majesty,' Cecil argued, 'as long as Mary is alive, there will be other attempts to place her on the throne, however innocent she may be of any such ambition.'

Elizabeth glared at Cecil. 'Cast your mind back a few years, Cecil. There was a time when I languished in the Tower because Wyatt and others sought to remove my sister from her throne in response to her insistence on marrying Philip of Spain. They claimed to act in my name without even consulting me — should I therefore have been taken out and beheaded, say you?'

'The circumstances are different, Majesty.'

'How? Tell me that, or remain silent!' Elizabeth snapped. When Cecil made no reply, she gestured him out of the Audience Chamber with an angry wave of her hand. 'Bring me a better case than this, before I will order the execution of a cousin and a rightful queen.'

'I will, Your Majesty,' Cecil assured her, 'once I have satisfied myself that any further intelligence that comes from her servant is not tainted by mischief.'

XVII

Elizabeth sat, open-mouthed and shaking slightly, as Cecil read out loud the long dispatch from Francis Walsingham in Paris, written originally in cipher and copied into readable form by one of the several cipher clerks employed by Cecil for that purpose. The news that it contained was devastating and had serious implications for future English foreign policy.

Put shortly, there had been a massive massacre of Protestants in France. On the eve of the Feast of Saint Bartholomew, only days after the marriage of the Catholic royal princess Margaret of Valois to the Protestant Henry of Navarre in what many had hoped would be an end to the religious wars in France, up to thirty thousand 'Huguenot' Calvinist Protestants had been slaughtered. It had begun in Paris, allegedly on orders that originated in the Palace, and had spread around the country like a fast-moving forest fire.

Cartloads of Protestant corpses had been heaved into the Seine, but a small handful of those who had survived, mainly those of a noble or wealthy origin, were currently experiencing a nervous sanctuary in the Paris home of the English Ambassador Walsingham, who to judge by the tone in which his dispatch had been written was clearly traumatised by the entire affair and was pleading to be recalled to London.

When Cecil had finished, he found Elizabeth staring into his eyes with the same look of helpless innocence that she had displayed on her first day as Queen, and he realised that for all her bravado and occasional cruelty towards those who frightened her, she was still the same girl whose service he had entered all those years ago and he softened.

'You wish to know what I would advise you to do?' he asked gently.

She nodded. 'Yes please, Cecil, but not the death of Mary this time, since she surely had nothing to do with it.'

'No, Majesty, and if anything quite the contrary. We must unite with all those nations that can assist in stemming the flow of Catholic violence and we must lead the Protestant opposition to it.'

'How?'

'An alliance, first of all, between England and those in France who have always protected the Huguenots, even though Catholic themselves. Then a further alliance with the Low Countries, with the objective of assisting them to throw off the Spanish yoke.'

'I know you well enough to see by your face that there is something further that you fear to advise me,' Elizabeth commented, almost playfully, and Cecil nodded, his head bowed.

'I have remained silent on the matter for several years now, but it may no longer be avoided, given the slow creep of time, even though it does not reflect itself in Your Majesty's natural beauty,' Cecil lied, bracing himself for the angry rebuke that never came.

'Nevertheless, I remain unmarried and without an heir,' Elizabeth said tauntingly, aware of what Cecil was working his way around to with fear in the pit of his stomach. 'You wish me yet again to consider marriage, do you not?'

Cecil almost sagged with relief as he looked back into Elizabeth's eyes, in which the mischievous twinkle of old had returned, as if someone had managed to wind back the calendar by twenty years.

'Tell me, Cecil,' she goaded him further, 'given that I am now in my thirty-ninth year, which of the available Protestant princes of Europe would contemplate taking such an old lady into his bed? And should he do so and should his seed perform its allotted task, do you seriously propose that I risk childbirth, as did my sister before me, only to die in the attempt?'

'Your sister did not die in childbirth, Your Majesty.'

'She died of an affliction brought on by it,' Elizabeth insisted. 'But do not avoid my first question, Cecil — who would have me in my old age?'

'There is the young Francis, Duke of Alençon, Your Majesty. He is of royal blood, being the youngest of Queen Dowager Catherine's sons. He is third in line to the throne of France currently occupied by his older brother Charles. It wants only his death and the death of the next in line Henri and Francis will be King of France.'

'That is rather a lot of deaths between him and the throne, Cecil,' Elizabeth chuckled, 'so I must assume that he is young enough to outlive them all. How old is this Francis, exactly?'

'He is currently seventeen,' Cecil told her as he swallowed hard, 'but of all the sons of Catherine he is the most lenient towards the Huguenots.'

'So he is a Catholic himself?' Elizabeth chortled at Cecil's obvious discomfort and Cecil nodded, while closing his eyes in anticipation. 'So, if I have this correctly summarised,' Elizabeth continued dismissively, 'you are proposing that I entertain an offer of marriage, should it eventuate, from a man less than half my age who is a Catholic and whose mother detests England with a passion? The former brother-in-law of the Scots Mary? And a man whose youthful vigour, either in the marital bed, or in consequence of it, would get me with child

157

and thereby expose me to the perils of childbirth at an age at which few women have been known to survive it? Have I omitted anything pertinent in that assessment of what you propose and would it really be in England's best interests?'

'It would ally England with a man who, when he becomes King of France, would be favourable towards Protestants, Your Majesty.'

'And should I marry him and die without issue, England would fall to France as part of its wider empire, thereby returning us back to the days when we were simply an outpost of Normandy,' Elizabeth reminded him. 'Is there really no-one else?'

'Not abroad, Majesty, so far as I have been able to ascertain.'

Elizabeth's eyebrows rose in challenge. 'And here in England? You have tactfully eluded any reference to Robert Dudley, who would marry me by crawling across broken glass, given the slightest opportunity. Why do you not suggest him?'

Cecil blanched and shook his head. 'He has many enemies at Court and the suspicions regarding the death of his first wife remain. I fear that were you to marry him, the nation would be in uproar, both Catholic and Protestant. The Protestants because they despise him for the favour you have ever shown him and the Catholics in order to shake your grip on your crown.'

'Enough of these games, Cecil,' Elizabeth hissed as her face hardened. 'You may advise Walsingham that he has my blessing to return to Court only if he brings with him this young buck of Alençon who you would lever into my affections. It would cheer me immensely to have a young gallant chasing my farthingale, but be advised privily that I will never marry him. Indeed, having survived this far without marriage, I doubt that I will ever marry anyone. Say rather that

I am married to my people. And now I bid you a good morning, since I have an appointment with a physician regarding the state of my teeth. No doubt his advice, as usual, will be as unwelcome as yours.'

Elizabeth and Robert Dudley strolled, her hand on his arm, through the specially created garden whose recently planted, but fully mature, rhododendron blooms glistened in the glow cast up periodically by the exploding firework displays across the great lake that had taken a week to set up. They were heading for the Great Hall of Kenilworth Castle and the twelfth banquet in a row in honour of their royal visitor. Earlier in the day they had sat enthralled on special platforms on the shore of the recently commissioned artificial lake and watched a splendid masque featuring a moving dolphin made entirely of paper treated with a clear tar, in the belly of which a small orchestra had played some of Elizabeth's favourite tunes from her youth. Tomorrow would consist of a morning hunt, followed by afternoon bear-baiting, then more masques at yet another banquet.

'This must have cost more than my entire Exchequer is worth,' Elizabeth said as she snuggled in closer and slid her hand down so that it could grasp his. 'The members of the Court are all jealous and I have heard unworthy rumours that you financed it all by joining Captain Drake in his raids on Spanish bullion ships.'

Robert laughed gently, looked round cautiously, then kissed her on the cheek, recoiling slightly from the smell of whiskey on her breath and the residual taste of ceruse on his lips. 'In truth, Master Drake has only recently returned from his journey to the ends of the world, and those of us who were far-sighted enough to invest in his enterprise have been well rewarded. He has also caused Philip of Spain to rage at his own mariners for allowing it to happen.'

'Summon Master Drake to Court once we are back at Whitehall,' Elizabeth requested as watched a massive explosion of red stars across the lake spelling out 'E.R.' in gold letters in its centre. 'I am flattered that you spent all your gains on such a splendid retreat for me from all the cares of running the nation. It's a pity that Cecil was not well enough to share it.'

'Indeed, but I had a reason of my own for inviting you down here,' Robert murmured.

'You wish to enter my good books in order to acquire yourself forgiveness for something wicked that you have done?' she asked teasingly, then dropped her gentle pace down the path as Robert stopped still and pulled her towards him with his hand until they were only inches apart.

'Dearest Lillibet,' he whispered, 'I have organised all this as a final reminder of how much you have always owned my heart, and in the hope that you will finally favour me with your hand in marriage.'

'Away, Robert!' she giggled nervously. 'The young girl you held so tenderly in the copse at Hatfield has become an old hag with a pockmarked face and shaky teeth.'

'To me the years have stood still,' Robert insisted, 'and when I look at you, it is as if we are still lying in the sweet grass together — or, more recently, on a bolster in Whitehall.'

'Hush, Robert!' she urged him. 'Those matters must remain our secret, if England is to acquire allies.'

'A secret, in particular, from that ugly little French dwarf with the oily manners and the complexion of a marsh toad?'

'I assume you are referring to Duke Francis of Alençon — and more recently of Anjou, since his brother Henry became King of France?'

'Yes, your "Frog" as you call him. Do you pretend to insult him as a secret sign of your passion for him?'

'Fie, Robert!' Elizabeth chuckled. 'He is half my age and yours, and if I feel anything for him it is as an aunt towards a gallant little nephew. As for pet names being a sign of my affections, I must indeed be promiscuous with them, since I call Cecil "Spirit" and his son Robert "Pigmy". Do I not also call you my "Eyes"?'

'I would be more to you than mere eyes,' Robert replied almost pleadingly as he leaned in to kiss her and she averted her face, then pulled him back into their casual stroll as Blanche Parry, several yards behind them, looked discreetly up at another burst of fireworks.

In the silence that followed Robert was clearly deep in thought and his voice, when he reclaimed the conversation, was more business-like in its tone.

'You referred to our ages and you must know that I need an heir for all the riches that I have accumulated. For this I must marry.'

'And this I forbid, Robert, as you must know,' Elizabeth replied stiffly. 'If the true purpose of this splendid two weeks was to secure my consent to your marriage to another, then it is withheld. If I may not marry, then neither may you.'

'So we grow old together and neither of us will have anyone to leave our estates to?'

Robert responded with a sigh when Elizabeth nodded and confirmed his fear.

'At least we shall grow old in each other's company, as we have always been for as long as I can remember. As for the succession to the English throne, it will most likely travel north to Scotland. Although not to that false cousin of mine who seeks my overthrow with Catholic intrigue. If she is not more careful, and were I not so merciful, she would by now be feeding the worms. And talking of feeding, I trust that you commanded sugared almonds?'

XVIII

There was much bustle and excitement on the Plymouth quayside as Elizabeth walked carefully down the gangplank of the Golden Hind on the arm of the French Ambassador de Marchaumont, who was smiling broadly at the honour being bestowed upon him of participating in what was to follow. He was naïve enough to believe that it was a personal recognition of the regard in which he was held by England's Queen, when in fact he was being kept sweet on the recommendation of Walsingham, who was using his offices in an attempt to negotiate a treaty with his King that would oblige the French to intervene on behalf of the Dutch in their ongoing attempts to throw off the Spanish yoke. Added to which, the overt endorsement by France of the honouring of the man reviled by Spain as a pirate would serve as a fart in the face of Philip II.

Francis Drake was waiting on the foredeck, dressed in a new doublet and fresh hose and with a triumphant grin on his sunblackened face as he knelt in homage. He had much to grin about, having returned late the previous year after a masterly feat of seamanship in navigating the entire globe. In the process he had lost four of his ships, but had successfully entered the Pacific around the Magellan Strait of South America, then attacked the Spanish ships and ports that he found on the far coast. Loaded with looted gold and other precious cargoes, he had finally made his way back to Plymouth via the Cape of Good Hope. He was now reviled by Philip of Spain, who had named him 'El Diablo', but was about to be rewarded by the only monarch who mattered to him.

Elizabeth handed the ceremonial sword to de Marchaumont, with terse instruction as to how it was to be employed when she nodded. Drake was still kneeling, his eyes firmly on the gently rolling deck, as Elizabeth intoned 'Arise, Sir Francis Drake' and the French Ambassador dubbed each of his doublet shoulders as instructed. A rousing cheer from the mariners on deck was echoed by the excited crowds on the quayside and it was all over. England had a new naval champion.

Back in Whitehall Palace, Elizabeth was rapidly adjusting to the many changes in personnel that had been ordained by circumstances. Her trusted Senior Lady, Blanche Parry, was some years older than her mistress and in her early seventies was beginning to fall prey to the many fevers and other contagions that crept into the royal palaces via the menials who delivered food and other goods, and she was regularly excused her duties due to ill health. In her absence Elizabeth Hardwick, Countess of Shrewsbury, was doing her best to shepherd the other Queen's Ladies in their many and varied duties of attendance on their royal mistress, but Elizabeth missed the confidences she was able to share with her old friend and companion Blanche.

There was another significant absentee from the high-born attendants on all formal occasions. Lettice Knollys, Countess of Essex, had been widowed the previous year, when her husband Walter Devereux had returned from serving the Queen in Ireland with a severe flux that had eventually proved fatal. There were rumours of poison, but whatever the cause of Walter's death, Lettice had been left to supervise the raising of her eleven-year-old son Robert, now the 2nd Earl of Essex. Elizabeth had recognised her years of faithful attendance upon her by granting her leave to absent herself from Court whenever the need arose and she was now rarely to be seen a few feet behind the Queen whenever the Court was summoned.

But while Elizabeth could afford to dispense with two of her favourite Ladies, she found the regular absences through ill health of Cecil much harder to abide. For some years now he had been 'Baron Burghley', in honour of his years of devoted service, but his elevation had proved to be no protection against his increasing inability to walk or stand for any length of time, and his breathlessness even when seated was something that Elizabeth found particularly distressing, since it reminded her that she was getting no younger herself and the aches in her own bones were a daily reminder that her reign would not last for ever.

Partly in deference to his growing frailty, and in the hope that reduced duties might prolong the years in which he could still give sage advice, Elizabeth had appointed Francis Walsingham as a companion Secretary of State, and had agreed to Cecil's son Robert, that curious and solemn little hunchback, carrying out most of the routine clerical work that his father would once have supervised down to the last vellum. Between them Walsingham and Robert Cecil kept the ship of state afloat and she did not lack able support in matters of correspondence and diplomacy.

Perhaps the hardest to bear was the almost continual absence of her beloved Robert, with whom an almost brotherly friendship had existed these past forty years and more. He was said to be constantly brooding in his castle of Kenilworth, adding to its fortifications, extending its gardens or improving its moat. He seemed to have accepted with good grace that he would never be her husband and given their long and happy association Elizabeth was content to allow him to lick his wounds behind the walls of the magnificent stronghold that was the seat of his earldom.

In any case, she was not short of Courtly attention for as long as Francis of Anjou was by her side. Her devoted 'Frog', far from taking offence at his nickname, seemed to delight in being on such familiar terms with the Queen of England and while their respective ambassadors were still walking carefully around plans for the two to marry, neither of them was in any great hurry. Elizabeth was twice his age and he was no great specimen of Courtly manhood, given his dark countenance, which at least hid most of the pockmarks that were the legacy of a childhood bout of smallpox and the slight curvature of the spine which, although not as marked as that of Robert Cecil, tended to accentuate his natural lack of height. Height was regarded as one of the essential attributes of handsome men and Robert Dudley never lost an opportunity to pepper his many quarrels with both Francis and Robert Cecil with references to their lack of it. Dear Robert, always jealous of other men by her side; it was perhaps as well that he was absent from Court most of the time, since dear fawning Frog was never far from her extended hand when she invited a chaste kiss from him.

Her reverie was interrupted by the announcement of the entry of Walsingham, and it occurred to Elizabeth yet again that she had so far not bestowed a nickname on him. This was perhaps because his stern demeanour at all times seem to prohibit it, and she was mentally toying with 'Ferret' when he bowed and sought permission to address her in that formal and somewhat quaint, way of his.

'By all means, Sir Francis. Is it a Privy Seal matter, or have you unearthed yet more conspirators against the throne?'

'Possibly the latter, Your Majesty,' Walsingham confirmed as he took the seat next to hers into which she had waved him. 'I have, as you requested, maintained many contacts in France, since we hope for an alliance with them against the Spanish who continue to occupy the Netherlands without challenge. Through a friendly Catholic source in Paris I have been advised that the Pope has commissioned and financed, the establishment of seminaries throughout that nation for the training of priests.'

'And why should it concern England if the Bishop of Rome wishes to add to his deluded servants and the French are misguided enough to play host to them?'

'It seems that the priests they are training are then being smuggled into England, to continue to celebrate the heathen Mass in the private houses of those who have — and forgive me, but perhaps unwisely — been allowed to continue to worship in their own wicked way.'

'You believe my tolerance of other forms of worship to have been abused?'

'Put bluntly and with the greatest respect to both yourself and my Lord Burghley who advised it at the time, that would seem to be the case. While respect for freedom of religion is a matter that does Your Majesty great credit, it can — if abused — lead to the encouragement of further plots against Your Majesty's person. The earlier risings in the north and most notably the treasonous plotting of the Duke of Norfolk, could not have occurred without overwhelming Catholic support. And then, of course, there is the matter of the Scots Mary.'

Elizabeth tutted. 'You begin to sound like Cecil, my dear Walsingham, forever bending my ear to have my cousin executed. And for what, precisely? Bring me evidence that she is behind these plots and not merely their inspiration and I will remove her head. Until then I must give her the benefit of the doubt.'

'I did not come here this morning to press the matter of Mary of Scotland, Your Majesty,' Walsingham explained as tactfully as he could. 'Rather I seek your authority to smoke out these Catholic invaders in whichever households they may be located.'

'Indeed, you have my blessing for that,' Elizabeth said. 'But once you have smoked them out, do you propose to turn the smoke into flame and burn them as heretics?'

Walsingham smiled grimly as he contemplated that prospect, but then resumed his noncommittal expression as he pointed out the disadvantages of such a policy. 'The people of Smithfield would recoil from further exposure to burning human flesh, Your Majesty. Added to which, it might then be argued that we had returned to the horrors of your late sister's reign and that you are no better than her.'

'What then, Walsingham?' Elizabeth demanded testily. 'Since I have rarely known you come to me with a problem without also being accompanied by its solution, what have you in mind?'

Walsingham smiled at the compliment and continued with enhanced confidence. 'Given that we may point to Catholic poison being at the root of previous rebellions, may we not enact legislation that makes the harbouring of such covert priests and their attempts to convert your loyal subjects to the heresies of Rome, in themselves acts of treason? Then you may have them taken onto Tower Green to entertain the mob with the traditional hanging, drawing and quartering.'

Elizabeth grimaced, then nodded quickly, as if wishing to end that part of the conversation. 'Yes, yes, do that — and with my approval. Is there anything else for this morning?'

'Yes — a related matter in many ways, Your Majesty. I wish to send agents of my selection into the Low Countries, in order to assess the plight of the Dutch and the strength of the Spanish troops that are imposed upon them. While there, it would be my instruction to them that they establish permanent contacts with those who work covertly for the overthrow of the Spanish, to arrange for various city gates to be thrown open to our forces when they invade.'

Elizabeth's initial reaction was a look of horror. 'As Privy Seal in all but name, you above all people must surely appreciate that we cannot afford to assemble an army at this time, however worthy the cause. And by intervening in the Netherlands we would be certain to provoke the Spanish, whose navy is well equipped to invade our shores.'

Walsingham smiled, somewhat condescendingly Elizabeth thought. 'Indeed, Majesty, I am well aware of our present inadequacy in the matter of foot soldiers. However, as for our navy, we can thank Hawkins and Drake for the increase in ships and do they not also provoke Philip of Spain by their acts of piracy?'

'Enough, Walsingham,' Elizabeth growled in the warning tone that every Courtier had learned to take good heed of. 'I will not have such fine gentlemen decried in my hearing. They bring great riches back to England by their brave efforts — riches that would otherwise be translated into yet more Spanish ships. You have my leave to enquire as to how matters progress in the Low Countries, but no further. Are we clearly understood on that point?'

'We are indeed, Your Majesty,' Walsingham replied deferentially as he rose and bowed his way out of the presence.

Down in the cluster of offices allocated to the Secretary of State, Cecil waved Walsingham into his company and called for wine to be served. Once the server was back out of earshot, he leaned across the desk and lowered his voice conspiratorially.

'I have reason to suspect another plot, Francis.'

Walsingham's eyes gleamed as he demanded further information and Cecil's face glowed with pride as he supplied them.

'Like your good self, I have spies in important quarters and through one of them I have succeeded in intercepting a letter from the new Spanish Ambassador, de Mendoza, to certain remaining Catholic sympathisers of the Scots Mary back in Scotland. It makes reference to plans for an element of the Scots to invade from the north, while French Catholics will land on the south coast.'

'I had believed the Auld Alliance to be at an end,' Walsingham replied.

Cecil nodded. 'And so it is, in its old form. But Catholics are Catholics, wherever they may be found and, as you yourself have learned, France has become the centre for the creation of new Jesuits who then sneak across the Channel, presumably by night, as the first wave of the new infestation. This cannot be occurring without the connivance and most certainly the knowledge, of the French Ambassador. Despite the recent honour bestowed upon him by Elizabeth, the slimy bastard is believed to be acting as the go-between for the French arm of an invasion that will be supported by Philip of Spain.'

'Dear God!' Walsingham whispered. 'If France and Spain unite to overthrow Elizabeth, using the influence of the Catholic faith, then we shall be hard put to resist it. Only a few moments ago the Queen was reminding me that we have no finances for an army!'

170

'Then we must employ other tactics, must we not?' Cecil replied with a grim smile. 'But you must brace yourself for ill tidings, my old friend. My spies have kept constant watch on the town house of the French Ambassador and of late he has entertained a frequent visitor. Francis Throckmorton.'

Walsingham whistled in surprise, then after a moment's reflection he nodded. 'I am not totally surprised to learn of that. While I was in Paris, serving under his uncle Nicholas, I had occasion to note his invariable association with and seeming friendship for, leading members of the Catholic Guise family. I thought it then to be part of some spying activity for his uncle, but it was equally possible that he was being converted and turned inside out to become a Catholic plotter. He is well placed to work like a worm in the soil now that he is back in England.'

'Not from where he is at present,' Cecil grimaced. 'I had him arrested in the early hours of this morning and as we speak he is no doubt confirming my suspicions to a gentleman in the Tower who is skilled in what he does and advised of what it is we wish to hear.'

Cecil's confidence in the sadistic talents of the Queen's tightener of the thumbscrews and rotator of the rack was fully vindicated within hours and the eager confession of the entire plot resulted in Throckmorton's execution and the expulsion of the second Spanish Ambassador in succession, coupled with a stern dispatch from Elizabeth that left Philip of Spain in no doubt that no replacement was required.

The 'Throckmorton Plot', as Cecil dubbed it, also resulted in a change of surroundings for Mary of Scotland. Still not convinced that her cousin was sufficiently isolated from residual Scottish sympathisers and obsessed with the need to keep her under the constant eye of a gaoler whose competence and loyalty were beyond suspicion, Elizabeth had in mind transferring her to the moated manor house at Chartley along with her latest guardian Amias Paulet, of whom Mary complained so often in her ill-tempered letters to Elizabeth that the latter concluded that Paulet must be performing his allocated duties with relish. As for Chartley itself, it possessed a deep moat and was even further into the depths of the English Midlands, twelve miles from Tutbury and still in Staffordshire. It also belonged to the young 2nd Earl of Essex, Robert Devereux, whose widowed mother was Lettice Knollys, one of the Queen's longest serving ladies.

Elizabeth outlined her proposal to the two Cecils, father and son, as they sat at supper with her in her Withdrawing Chamber at Whitehall. William Cecil nodded. 'Your judgment is excellent, as always, Your Majesty, but wherever Mary is lodged she will continue to be an inspiration to Catholic rebels and viewed from across the Channel, one county of England is much the same as another.'

'But the further from the sea, or from any large town with adequate supply sources and signposts, the better, surely?'

'Indeed, Majesty,' William Cecil conceded, as his son Robert looked up mischievously from the roast pig from which he was carving.

'All the same, Your Majesty,' Robert chimed in, 'one has to hope that the son obeys Your Majesty with greater loyalty than his mother.'

His father shot him an angry look, but it was too late.

'Your meaning?' Elizabeth asked.

'You do not allow your Ladies to marry, is that not the case?'

'Not without my consent, certainly not,' Elizabeth confirmed. 'But Lady Exeter — Lettice Knollys — is now a widow, is she not?'

'I'm sorry,' Robert Cecil replied with a well feigned expression of regret, 'I had of course assumed that you knew, but had chosen not to punish her, give her years of loyal service.'

'Punish her for what, young Cecil?' Elizabeth demanded with irritation. 'She is no longer a widow, say you?'

'Robert,' his father murmured in warning, but there was no stopping Robert Cecil now that he had an old enemy in his sights. He looked across at Elizabeth and replied, 'She has indeed remarried, Your Majesty. She is now the Countess of Leicester.'

Elizabeth's entire frame went rigid as she dropped the marchpane heart onto the board, where symbolically it broke into two pieces. She appeared to be having a seizure as her breath came in tortured gasps, but when William Cecil rose from her side in an effort to assist her she pushed him angrily back and managed a few hoarse words.

'If you wish to serve me at this moment, Cecil, bring me Robert and Lettice. Tonight. And in chains!'

It was two days later, on a windy late afternoon, when Robert Dudley and Lettice stood, heads bowed and hands manacled, while Elizabeth's ranting abuse rang over their heads.

'Such ingratitude! Such disloyalty! Such — such — treason! What have you to say for yourselves, as if anything could justify your foul betrayal, before I have you consigned to the Tower?'

'I love him, my Lady,' Lettice muttered.

'Speak louder, if you dare!' Elizabeth commanded her. Lettice raised her head, her eyes blazing with defiance and yelled back at the top of her voice

'I said I love him, my Lady — even if it means my death!'

'And you?' Elizabeth demanded as her livid stare switched to Robert Dudley.

'I had never hoped in my entire life to love someone as thoroughly as I love my wife. And our union has already been blessed by God. Would you put a woman to death when she is carrying a child?'

'You married in secret, knowing that I would forbid it were you to seek my blessing. Is that not treasonous?'

'It has certainly proved to be foolhardy,' Robert said. 'But surely it is God alone who has the power to bless unions?'

'Do not be impertinent!' Elizabeth snapped, as her anger and grief threatened to overcome her completely. 'I will have you both held in strict confinement in one of the guest suites on the ground floor, until my ire has abated sufficiently to determine what shall be done with you. Were Lettice not with child, you would both be in the Tower. Now get out, the two of you!'

She swept from her throne as the two were led out, still manacled and ran through her Withdrawing Chamber to her Bedchamber, where she flung herself on her bolster fully clothed. Her wails and screams could be heard downstairs in the Privy Kitchen, into which Blanche Parry was summoned by anxious cooks and scullions. She listened only briefly to the agonised noises above her, before running up the service stairs to her mistress, who was barely conscious by the time that Blanche placed a comforting hand on her still heaving shoulder.

'I had no idea what a fool I had raised until I heard you open your big fat drivelling mouth!' William Cecil bellowed at his son as he stormed out into the garden of the family house a week later, when advised that Robert had returned from wherever he had been hiding from parental wrath. His father was accompanied by Francis Walsingham, whose drawn face registered his embarrassment at being obliged to hear such a tongue lashing. He had only agreed to accompany his friend and close companion Cecil, at his urging, when advised that if he did not, it was likely that Robert Cecil would die at his own father's hand.

'The Queen would have found out sooner or later,' Robert wheedled as he half hid behind a mature apple tree, 'and better that it come from one whose greatest value to Her Majesty is the extent of their privy knowledge.'

'When you have grown fit enough to continue in my service,' Cecil yelled back, 'you will have learned that there is both a time and a suitable opportunity to reveal one's knowledge. The Queen is said to have shut herself away for three days, refusing audience with all but Blanche Parry and none dare approach her even now, even with routine business.'

'And Leicester and his wife?' Robert asked, as his father's face grew even more crimson.

'That is why you dropped that burden on the Queen, was it not? Something else you must learn, before I again acknowledge you as having sprung from my loins, is that one never — never, mark you? — acts out of personal spite, but only for good cause. You will no doubt be disappointed to learn that the Earl and Countess of Leicester have merely been banned from Court and sent back in disgrace to Kenilworth.'

'So no great harm done, then,' Robert argued, as his father's face returned to something approaching its normal colour, although the tone of voice was still abrasive.

'No great harm to them, certainly, but I am no nearer solving a more pressing matter in a satisfactory way. I had hoped — until you ruined the entire supper — to persuade Her Majesty that this latest uncovered plot by Throckmorton left her with no choice but to have the Scots Mary put to death. Instead of which she has gone into some sort of mourning and cannot be persuaded to consider any issue of State, particularly one that has to do with a family member.'

'So what will you do?'

'Fortunately, as the old saying goes, there is more than one way to skin a cat. If Her Majesty wants direct proof of Mary's ill intentions towards her, then we shall have to encourage Mary to supply it in her own fair hand. This will require subtlety, which you appear not to possess in any quantity, even small, so Walsingham and I have devised a process that will not only not involve you, but will give you cause to smoulder with inner rage, since it will involve another man of whom you seem to have made an enemy. That is, assuming that we can find him.'

XIX

William Cecil stood in the open doorway and watched Tom Ashton, stripped to the waist and glistening with sweat, hammering at a plough share. Tom looked up as he became aware of Cecil's presence, then swore as he threw down the hammer.

'Come to arrest me, at a guess. Desertion from the royal service, or some other invented charge.'

'Nice to meet with you again also, Tom,' Cecil replied sarcastically. 'The last time I was here you were merely working the bellows for your sister's father-in-law, if I remember correctly. Now you seem to have come up in the world.'

'No thanks to you,' Tom growled. 'All that shit about rewarding me with an estate if I did your dirty work spying on the Scots Mary. I came back here, rather than court death on my own impoverished estate at Knighton. Just in time for Ted Bestwick to die and for my brother-in-law Allan Bestwick to take over the forge business here. He's teaching me all the skills I'll need to lead an honest life.'

'That will make a change,' Cecil said sardonically, 'but I didn't come all the way to Attenborough to arrest you. Nor do I need my horse shod, as I did last time.'

'Then what?' Tom asked as he picked up the hammer menacingly.

'I wish you to travel to where the Scots Mary is currently being held, in order to arrange her final downfall,' Cecil announced, to which Tom responded with a peal of bitter laughter.

'Ever the optimist — like your attempts to turn me into a clerk.'

Cecil sighed. 'It is your impulsive nature and your inability to think sideways, that will guarantee that you never progress in the Queen's service without suitable patronage. But this time it is I who can put you in the way of a bigger estate, should my information be correct. It is to test that information and by so doing persuade Her Majesty that Mary of Scotland should be put to death, that I require your resumed service. You will not be gone for too many weeks and if you return with success you will be the lord of an estate not far from your heart's desire, as it transpires.'

'It will be quite simple and requires only that you both play your part according to my instruction,' Cecil told Tom Ashton and Jenny Spittell, who Cecil had summoned to join them at an inn just outside Lichfield on the third night of their journey from Attenborough to Chartley. Walsingham had slipped without any discomfort or resentment into the secondary role allocated to him by Cecil and was content to receive his instructions in company with Tom and Jenny.

'Before Jenny slipped away from service at Chartley in order to accompany me to Attenborough on the pretence that she was visiting her sick mother,' Cecil explained, 'she was able to confirm the existence of what appears to be yet another plot to overthrow Queen Elizabeth and replace her with Mary. Apparently Mary is regularly receiving messages from supporters that are smuggled into the house in beer barrels; she has her own supply delivered directly, mainly for her male attendants, but unless they are all hopeless soaks the quantity consumed is suspicious.'

'Who supplies the beer and who is sending the messages?' Tom asked, already intrigued and with all thought of refusing further work for Cecil driven from his head now that he was back with Jenny.

Cecil smiled. 'That part was easy, since the gaoler Paulet raised his concerns with me over the expense involved and I had the brewer's premises watched. It soon became obvious that messengers were arriving in nearby Uttoxeter shortly before each weekly barrel delivery and it was then a simple matter of pouncing on the morning that a delivery was about to be made. We found a letter from a high noble called Babington sealed in a watertight package inside the bung of the barrel that was about to be delivered. It was in cipher, so it was hastily copied before the original was replaced and delivered. The cart driver was tortured, but steadfastly disclaimed any guilty knowledge. As for the brewer, he has been terrified into going along with our intended plan.'

'Which is?' Tom asked.

Cecil nodded to Walsingham, who took over. 'You are about to convert your trade into that of drayman,' he told Tom. 'As yet, according to Jenny, who has contrived to always be in the Lady Mary's company whenever a new barrel is sprung and who can therefore confirm what has been going on, Mary has never penned any reply to these letters, although she seems mightily pleased by their contents. So we shall employ a skilled forger to imitate Babington's hand and a cipher clerk to put it into the correct code, then you will deliver a new message that requires Mary's written assent to the vilest acts of treason. Jenny will then advise us as to whether or not there is any reply and we shall remove it from the barrel on your return. By doing so, we shall catch the wicked woman conspiring, by her own hand, in a plot to assassinate the Queen.'

'But there is no such plot?' Tom asked, horrified at the depth of deception to which Cecil was prepared to descend.

'Not at this time, no. But how soon before such a plot exists? Previous plots have all but encompassed Elizabeth's death and it is known that Babington has contacts with both the Court of Spain and the Catholic League in France. He will be no loss to England, and hopefully Elizabeth will be so enraged when she learns of what her cousin was prepared to put her name to that she will at long last order her execution. Then England shall be rid of Catholic plots for all time.'

'Back in Attenborough you made mention of an estate that will fall to me if we are successful,' Tom reminded Cecil, who nodded.

'The Babington family is extensive and has long established Yorkist roots that make them resentful of Tudor monarchs. They are Catholic to a man and they have many estates. When Babington falls, it will be necessary to arrest the family and one of their estates in Lincolnshire will then be transferred to you when all the estates fall to the Crown. I shall not require the Queen's consent to that, although no doubt she would give it, if consulted.'

'And then we can be married!' Jenny reminded Tom excitedly as all thought of refusal slipped from his conscience.

Three months later Mary Stuart went on trial for what amounted to treason for agreeing to a plan, in a letter that Babington had never sent, that would involve a joint invasion of England by Spanish and French troops, the capture and execution of Elizabeth and the placing of Mary herself on the throne of England. The outcome of that trial was never in doubt, with the execution of Babington a month previously having deprived Mary of any defence witness to deny the authenticity of the fateful letter that had provoked her gleeful response and with Walsingham among those on the jury who found her guilty.

Elizabeth was seen to be reluctant to sanction the death sentence and only relented when assured that it would be done cleanly, with an axe, and that her royal cousin would not be disembowelled in public like any other traitor. Mary was transferred to Fotheringhay Castle in Northamptonshire to await her execution and most of her entourage were cast out into the wilderness to find their own way back to Scotland. Mary Seton opted to remain until the very end, but graciously released Janet Spittell from her service when advised that her loyal attendant had met a local man who she wished to marry. The wedding bells duly rang out in St Mary's Church in Attenborough a few days ahead of the new Lord and Lady of an estate less than a day's ride from Jenny's former home taking up residence along with her overjoyed parents. The bridegroom at the service was now 'Sir' Thomas Ashton by dint of a ceremony in which Elizabeth had knighted a dozen men on the urging of Cecil, without any real knowledge of what they had done to earn the honour.

It took all of Cecil's persuasive skills to all but shame Elizabeth into signing the warrant for Mary's execution and even then on condition that it was not to be employed until she said so. When she continually avoided the subject at one Council meeting after another, Cecil risked his own neck by convening a meeting of Council when the Queen was on one of her regular tours of royal palaces while Whitehall was being thoroughly cleansed, and demanding that Council endorse the execution of the warrant. Mary was beheaded the following week and everyone ran for cover when the Queen shrieked her horror at what had happened at a volume that could be heard all over Windsor Castle.

However, she was drawn back into relying entirely on Cecil and her Council when responding to the assassination, the previous year, of Prince William of Orange, the leader of the Dutch resistance against the Spanish occupation force now commanded by the Duke of Parma and the surrender of yet more Dutch towns. When Parma laid siege to Antwerp and Philip of Spain signed an alliance with the Catholic League of France, Elizabeth was forced to be seen to do something and she had authorised Walsingham to negotiate the Treaty of Nonsuch, which committed England to supplying over six thousand foot soldiers and over one thousand cavalry to lift the siege of Antwerp. This was regarded by Philip of Spain as a declaration of war and Elizabeth now had to make good her promise. When Council agreed on the additional taxation of the nobility and merchants that would be required in order to finance the operation, Elizabeth was left with the task of selecting someone to command her forces and there was only one obvious person.

Robert Dudley had been grudgingly allowed back at Court a year previously, although his wife Lettice was still banned from attendance. Elizabeth had been touched to learn that their child had died in its infancy, but she still kept up an almost constant barrage of slights and insults whenever the name of her former Lady was mentioned. As for Robert himself, she was cool towards him, but thawed somewhat when he sought leave to introduce to Court his nineteen-year-old stepson Robert Devereux, 2nd Earl of Essex, already the epitome of a fine Tudor noble and anxious to win fame and fortune in battle.

The two Roberts presented themselves somewhat apprehensively in the Audience Chamber when summoned and as usual Elizabeth made great show of favour towards the handsome and excessively gallant stepson, while treating her former childhood companion as befitted a man in his mid-fifties who was past his prime and growing somewhat portly in self-satisfied middle age. In doing so, she was either forgetting that she herself was approximately the same age, with her years of youthful freshness well behind her, or was resentful of him because he reminded her so forcefully of her own fading beauty.

'You are presumably wondering why you have been summoned?' she demanded imperiously and as usual it was Essex with the ingratiating response.

'Any opportunity to be in Your Majesty's presence is welcome,' he oozed.

Elizabeth frowned slightly, then transferred her gaze to Robert. 'There was a time when I would have expected that sort of oily rejoinder from you, my lord of Leicester. But for once you may be of service to the nation.'

'How so, my Lady?' Robert asked with a studied failure to refer to 'Your Majesty'.

Elizabeth leaned towards her side table, lifted a document from it and waved it in the air. 'Walsingham, as you know, recently made this agreement with the Dutch, which requires us to lend them military aid and with particular reference to the re-taking of Antwerp from the Spanish oppressors. You are well known, and for some reason highly regarded, by our friends in the Low Countries and I am in the process of assembling a force to oppose the arrogance of the Duke of Parma. You may recall that it was on your insistence in Council that we offered aid to our Protestant friends in their time of need and it is therefore appropriate that you lead that force, along with your eager stepson here. The fleet that will transport you across the Channel is already assembling at Greenwich under your good friend Captain Hawkins, and you will leave whenever you have set your affairs in order.'

'Your Majesty does me great honour,' Robert replied coldly as he bowed, while Essex was almost quivering with excitement. 'We shall bring great glory for England, Your Majesty,' he cooed, 'and my father shall govern the Low Countries in your name.'

'He will do no such thing!' Elizabeth yelled, then glared back at Robert. 'I am well aware that you have already so ingratiated yourself with those who represent the United Provinces that they see you as their Governor-General. Be under no illusion that you are being dispatched over there to assume that role. Your duty to me will be solely to maintain a strong English military presence over there, to discourage any further inroads by the Spanish. I have no wish to rule over the Netherlands and even less do I wish to do so through the agency of yourself. Are we clearly understood on that point?'

'Indeed, my Lady,' Robert confirmed as he only half bowed. 'But,' he continued, 'has not Philip of Spain proclaimed that the signing of the Treaty of Nonsuch was a declaration of war against his nation? If that be the case and if we are to risk our lives in taking on the might of Spain, would it not be appropriate for me to assume some sort of generalship of the lands we shall be defending?'

'No it would not!' Elizabeth retorted hotly. 'Simply engage your men as a bulwark against further Spanish encroachment and do nothing to suggest that we are claiming the Netherlands for ourselves. Understood?'

'Understood,' Robert echoed, but Elizabeth's brow remained furrowed.

'Good. See to it that I am scrupulously obeyed in this. You are both now dismissed the presence.'

As they disappeared through the double doors that led back into the hallway her heart felt a pang of regret. She might well be sending Robert to his death and her last words to him had been curt and unloving. She took a deep breath and stiffened her resolve. Cecil had advised that they use the presence of English forces in the Low Countries as a bargaining counter with Philip of Spain and no more. She was obliged, for England's sake, to follow the sage advice of her tried and trusted adviser and not to fall prey to the urgings of her heart. She only hoped that Robert would return alive.

When he ultimately returned, it was in disgrace. The United Provinces were so heartened by the arrival at The Hague of a senior English noble with an armed force sent by Elizabeth that they persuaded Robert to accept the title of 'Governor-General'. He would always maintain that he had done so in Elizabeth's name, but even that ran contrary to her express instructions and she was furious. She expressed her fury in a letter to Robert personally, in which she reminded him of how he had been 'extraordinarily favoured by us above any other subject of this land' and went on to express her disbelief that he had 'in so contemptible a sort broken our commandment in a cause that so greatly touches us in honour.' This letter was hand delivered by an emissary, Sir Thomas Heneage, sent directly from London to The Hague and contained the command that Robert obey other instructions with which Heneage had been supplied, or 'you will answer the contrary at your utmost peril.'

Robert knew the wild rages of Elizabeth to be as dangerous as they sounded and was obliged to stand by meekly and deeply embarrassed, as Heneage read out, to a full assembly of the Council of State of the United Provinces, a further blast from the Queen of England dissociating herself and her nation from any form of governorship over the Netherlands and leaving no one in any doubt that the Earl of Leicester did not act with her authority. It was little wonder that Robert never again enjoyed any meaningful status in the region and after several military failures that were costing England money it did not have, during which Robert was obliged to pay and victual his troops at his own personal expense, he resigned his commission and returned to England greatly humiliated, but glad not to have been executed, such was Elizabeth's ire.

She was even more incensed when obliged to make peace terms with the Duke of Parma, thereby further revealing England's critical weakness on the ground. This gave further incentive to Philip of Spain to invade England and put paid for all time to the Protestant thorn in the Habsburg side. He would finally revenge himself on the woman who had arrogantly rejected his hand in marriage and at the same time could return England to the Pope. All it needed was a naval force sufficient to ferry Parma's land force across the Channel in pursuit of England's ragged, dysfunctional and demoralised army.

XX

England was now in greater peril than it had been since the Norman invasion. Elizabeth's grandfather Henry VII had put an end to private armies in the hope of preventing any further dynastic wars among the Plantagenets and her father Henry had all but bankrupted the nation by maintaining a royal army during his bitter squabbles with Francis of France. Cecil and others had constantly warned against the burden of taxation that would be imposed on the nobility were England to keep professional warriors in reserve against the prospect of wars that could be avoided with the appropriate diplomacy — another of Henry VII's policies — but the net result of such parsimony was that England had no well drilled and experienced force with which to ward off any Spanish invaders.

They were glumly considering their options as they sat around the Council table and as usual Her Majesty seemed to be assuming that someone had the answer and was keeping it from her out of personal animosity. She glared up the table to its far end, where Cecil and Walsingham sat like old men at a funeral party.

'Well, Cecil? What have you to suggest?'

The tired old man shook his head. 'I am no soldier, Your Majesty, but it would seem that if Philip of Spain succeeds in transporting the Duke of Parma's forces across the Channel, we would be hard put to beat them back.'

'I am no soldier either, Cecil,' Elizabeth replied coldly, 'but even I could have reached that conclusion. Does no-one have any idea as to how we might meet this threat?'

'Clearly they cannot be allowed to cross to England,' Walsingham offered, to a responding snort from Elizabeth. 'Perhaps one of my Counsellors could advise me of something of which I was not already aware,' she added.

It fell silent until Robert Dudley cleared his throat in Walsingham's defence. 'He speaks truer than you give him credit for, Your Majesty. The defence of this realm must be by sea.'

'Your pirate friends Hawkins and Drake?' Elizabeth asked. 'They have served England well by plundering Spanish treasure ships, but can they take on those massive floating cities that the Spanish employ to transport their soldiers?'

'We will not know until they are commanded to try, Your Majesty,' Robert pointed out. 'I would undertake to carry your commission down to Plymouth, assess the number of ships they have, along with their armament capability, then report back to this Council.'

'And sneak safely out of England on one of their vessels?' Robert Cecil asked with raised eyebrows.

'Silence, Pygmy!' Elizabeth retorted instinctively as she heard her beloved Robert being depicted as a coward. 'When you begin to demonstrate that you have inherited your father's wisdom, you may then — and only then — cast aspersions on others. My lord of Leicester is one of the few fighting men that this nation may call upon in its hour of dire need and I am minded to appoint him to command such land forces as we may still possess. Robert, consider yourself England's 'Lieutenant and Captain-General of the Royal Armies and Companies'. As for you, Pygmy, if you would prefer your head to remain on your shoulders, no more from you.'

'The matter of a naval force to prevent Philip's forces arriving here?' Walsingham asked in the hope of steering matters back to something more immediate and practical and Elizabeth nodded. 'Do you carry out the actions that Leicester proposed and bring us back the latest intelligence on the readiness of our ships to do battle with Spain.'

Walsingham nodded his agreement and shortly afterwards the Council was dismissed, with instructions to reconvene whenever Elizabeth commanded it.

Ten days later Walsingham was back seeking audience, which he was granted within minutes of it being requested. Elizabeth sat anxiously awaiting his report and waved her hand for him to sit next to her as she granted permission to speak. Walsingham was smiling, which was not only unusual, but hopefully a good sign.

'There is heartening news from Plymouth, Your Majesty. Sir John Hawkins, as your Navy Treasurer, has commissioned and equipped a whole new fleet of sleeker, faster ships that can come alongside the taller Spanish galleons and below the level of their gunsights. He hopes by this means to go among the enemy's vessels and send them to the bottom before the men they carry can grapple his ships and leap aboard, which is apparently the way the Spanish fight.'

'Good news indeed, Walsingham,' Elizabeth replied. 'But are we still outnumbered?'

'We will probably always be outnumbered, Majesty, but it is not the number of ships that will be crucial, or so Hawkins advises me. It is how they are deployed and to what purpose. In addition, Sir Francis Drake has already set sail for Spain, where he plans to attack those ships that Philip has already assembled in the port of Cadiz. He has in mind setting fire to vessels of his own and steering them into the port of Cadiz, where Philip's ships will be tightly packed and unable to cast off in time to prevent the fire from spreading.'

To Walsingham's surprise and consternation, Elizabeth frowned. 'There must be no suggestion that Drake does this on my command. We are still hopeful of negotiating our way out of this threat posed by Spain and Drake's actions — whether successful or not — would not assist those negotiations were it believed that the destruction of Spanish warships was anything other than an act of personal and piratical revenge by Drake.'

Walsingham's face fell. 'I doubt that Drake's fleet could be called back at this late stage — he was three days gone when I left Plymouth.'

'I did not say that I wanted his venture called off, Walsingham — simply that I do not wish my name associated with it. Now, say you that Hawkins has the main fleet commissioned? Is it adequately equipped? Men? Victuals? Gunpowder?'

Walsingham swallowed hard and chose the most diplomatic answer that came to him. 'The Navy revenues are all but depleted by the need to build the ships, Your Majesty. They have no shortage of men, but as for victuals — and particularly gunpowder — perhaps more taxation?'

'Out of the question! They must fight with what they have.'

'Yes, Majesty. I forgot to add that I have ordered the strengthening of the defences at Dover, although my lord of Leicester inclines towards the opinion that should the Spanish evade our sea defences, they will come at us up the Thames.'

'Leave land strategies to Robert Dudley,' Elizabeth replied, 'although your work at Dover was well thought. I have two more matters on which I require your counsel. The first is who is to command the English fleet and the second is how we on land are to be advised of how matters progress at sea, should it come to that.'

'As to the latter, Majesty, I have commissioned a series of faggot stacks along the high points of our southern counties. If and when the Spanish fleet is spied, each stack will be lit and act as a beacon that alerts those next along the cliffs to keep a close watch out to sea. The series of beacon fires will also alert our ground troops to the progress of the invasion force.'

Elizabeth frowned again. 'Our best intelligence is that the Spanish flotilla is intended only as transport for Parma's forces in the Low Countries. It is from there that the attack will come, if our sturdy mariners cannot prevent it. Which brings us back to my first question — who shall command our Navy?'

'I had thought Hawkins, Majesty — or perhaps Drake?'

Elizabeth shook her head. 'I will not have it said that in its hour of greatest challenge England could do no better than commission pirates to defend it. By all means grant line commissions to Hawkins and Drake — if he survives his rash venture in Cadiz — but which of our leading nobles has experience at sea?'

Walsingham lifted his bonnet back far enough to scratch his head for a moment, but while he was still thinking Elizabeth supplied the answer to her own question.

'I have in mind our cousin Charles Howard, Earl of Nottingham. He is but recently appointed Lord High Admiral and he was a sailor during his early life. Let it be proclaimed throughout the realm that our brave fleet shall be commanded by Lord Howard of Effingham — but for preference let him know first.'

Walsingham rose, then bowed his acquiescence as he backed towards the chamber door. Just before he reached it, Elizabeth had one more command.

'Ask the Earl of Leicester to attend upon me.'

An hour later Robert was ushered into the presence and as he bowed and doffed his bonnet, beads of sweat flew from the top of his greying hair.

Elizabeth smiled. 'Does my Master of Horse no longer enjoy the boundless energy of youth?'

'In truth, my dearest Lady, I ran all the way from the royal stables upon being advised that you wished to see me. Have I displeased you yet again?' he added with the boyish smile that looked somehow incongruous on his well-lined face.

'Not that I am aware,' Elizabeth replied. 'Sit by me here and perhaps take my hand for longer than is proper, then tell me how you fare in defending me from Philip of Spain.'

Robert preened as he took her hand, kissed it and proudly announced what he had so far achieved. 'I have sent word to every shire in the land for their trained bands to be dispatched to Tilbury, where a great earthwork is currently being raised. I hope to have almost twenty thousand men encamped behind it before the first Spanish sail is sighted in the Thames.'

'You are aware that Walsingham has ordered the strengthening of Dover?' Elizabeth asked.

Robert smiled condescendingly. 'With the greatest of respect to Sir Francis, he is no soldier. Were I invading England, I would not attempt to march a massive army for two days over land, with all the baggage and supplies that they would require, not to mention the need to lay waste to the surrounding countryside, when I could sail that army directly into London by way of one of the world's greatest rivers. They will come, if at all, up the Thames and we must be ready to repel them at Tilbury, with all the ordinance we can muster. But I am advised that the Tower Armoury lacks gunpowder and that such as exists has been requisitioned for the Navy.'

'Since the Navy is our first line of defence, then it is appropriate, is it not, that it be the first to receive such explosive as we have available?'

'And if the Navy fails?' Robert asked.

'I will give you the same command that I gave to Walsingham with regard to the Navy — your men must fight with what they have.'

They all waited, and waited, for Spanish sails to appear off the Lizard on England's most south westerly peninsular, then came news that Drake had succeeded in his bold plan to 'singe the King of Spain's beard'. The English privateer's fireships had made a bonfire of most of the original fleet moored in Cadiz Harbour and by way of an encore Drake had harassed a few coastal villages, then intercepted a Spanish treasure ship on its way back to port and made the proceeds available for the acquisition of more gunpowder. But they all knew that they had merely bought more time in which Robert Dudley could add to the defences at Tilbury, where a proud array of guns was now elevated to deliver fusillades of shot into the mid channel of the Thames. However, none of them as yet had anything to fire.

Then, in mid July 1588, word came of the lighting of the first of Walsingham's beacons, as the western horizon was filled with the white billowing sails of the largest fleet of ships that had ever been seen approaching the entrance to the English Channel. The massive troop carriers, crammed with grappling crews who would leap onto any English vessel that came close enough, resembled small towns with high sterns and the fleet had been organised into a massive crescent shape, with lightly armed carracks escorting the stately galleons in a fleet so extensive that it had taken two full days to sail out of Corunna. On board were eight thousand sailors and eighteen thousand soldiers and the total of one hundred and thirty ships marked the end product of Philip of Spain's obsessive drive to rebuild his fleet after Drake's earlier exploits. The Spanish were coming and they meant England no kindness.

Once the beacon was lit above Beachy Head in Sussex, Robert hustled Elizabeth behind the walls of Windsor Castle and from there they received regular second-hand accounts of the progress of the Armada up the Channel by fast horse-born relay messengers. As they all sat at supper, Elizabeth turned accusingly towards Walsingham and demanded to know how the Spanish had apparently slipped past Howard, Drake and Hawkins.

'I am no sailor, Majesty,' he replied with a worried frown, 'but it seems likely that they will make landfall somewhere in Flanders and from there will be able to load a second army for the assault on England.'

'Thank God we are ready for them at Tilbury,' Robert responded wearily, 'but at the last muster we had only four thousand men. Heaven forfend that the Spanish manage to come ashore and to prevent that we need ordinance for our cannon, to blow them out of the water.'

'Perhaps we should fire some of these lamprey dumplings at them,' Elizabeth replied.

'Or perhaps force the Spanish to eat them,' Robert jested back, 'for the dear Lord knows I cannot.'

A few days later came the dreaded news that the Spanish fleet had moored off the coast at Dunkirk and was now awaiting the transfer of Parma's huge and battle-hardened land army onto flat bottomed barges that could be steered through the shallows to the waiting Spanish galleons at anchor. They were not to know that Drake was about to do what he did best and send his feared 'hellburner' fire ships into the moored fleet, causing the Armada vessels to cut their anchors and allowing the stiff south-westerly to blow them aimlessly up the east coast of England. Nor were they advised that Dutch mariners had come to their aid, with their shallow draught 'flyboats' harassing every Spanish barge that tried to leave the small harbour of Gravelines.

It was therefore with a heavy heart that Robert sought audience with Elizabeth, in order to advise her that their only hope was to remove such gunpowder as remained in the storage houses at the Tower, load it into his cannons at Tilbury, then rely on the pathetic handful of 'trained band' militia currently behind the massive earth bank to race out and finish off any Spaniards who survived.

'It will be a hopeless act of self-sacrifice, will it not?' Elizabeth responded listlessly.

'You recall our nursery days, when we learned of the exploits of your forebears and most notably the fifth Henry? How he grabbed victory against all the odds in battles such as that at Agincourt? And before him, the great Edward, at Crecy? It is not superiority of arms that makes Englishmen the finest fighters in the world, my Lady — it is their courage and their refusal to be defeated.'

Elizabeth leaned forward and kissed Robert on the lips. 'Perhaps I should have married you, after all,' she conceded, 'since you are a man worthy of maintaining that great heritage.'

'And why not a woman?' Robert challenged her. 'If we are to send so many brave Englishmen to their deaths, are they not at least entitled to hear words of encouragement from their Queen?'

When Elizabeth looked blank, Robert took both her hands in his and gazed into her eyes. 'Come with me to Tilbury and address your army. At least we shall go down with words of defiance echoing across the Thames.'

'By God and I shall!' Elizabeth replied as the determination and obstinacy that had dominated her younger years somehow transfused her face with a flickering flame of her former beauty. 'Give orders for my horse to be saddled and do you accompany me. You are, after all, still my Master of Horse, even if I could not make you my husband.'

Late that afternoon four thousand apprehensive men gazed in astonishment as a small party of Tower Yeomen rode through the gateway of their fortress mound constructed entirely of Essex clay and announced in loud voices that they should prepare to greet their Queen. To a man they went down on one knee to the sight of Elizabeth, with battle armour strapped over her rich gown, being led into the centre of the drilling square on her grey palfrey by a middle aged, bareheaded, man on foot, who was holding her horse's bridle. A cry of acknowledgement went up as they recognised their commander, the Earl of Leicester, and watched him assist the Queen to dismount, then lead her by the hand to the platform from which drilling sergeants usually stood to supervise daily training.

Elizabeth removed her French hood and loosened her hair so that it fell in dark red folds onto the specially tailored armour that had been awaiting its first public appearance for many months now. She threw back her head, cleared her throat, then let her eyes roam across the long ranks of still kneeling men as her voice rang out clearly though the breeze generated by the incoming tide and above the cawing clamour of the sea birds.

'My loving people, we have been persuaded by some that are careful of our safety, to take heed how we commit ourselves to armed multitudes for fear of treachery; but, I do assure you, I do not desire to live to distrust my faithful and loving people. Let tyrants fear, I have always so behaved myself, that under God I have placed my chiefest strength and safeguard in the loyal hearts and goodwill of my subjects; and, therefore, I am come amongst you as you see at this time, not for my recreation and disport, but being resolved, in the midst and heat of battle, to live or die amongst you all — to lay down for my God and for my kingdoms and for my people, my honour and my blood even in the dust. I know I have the body of a weak and feeble woman; but I have the heart and stomach of a king — and of a King of England too, and think foul scorn that Parma or Spain, or any prince of Europe, should dare to invade the borders of my realm; to which, rather than any dishonour should grow by me, I myself will take up arms — I myself will be your general, judge and rewarder of every one of your virtues in the field. I know already, for your forwardness, you have deserved rewards and crowns and, we do assure you, on the word of a prince, they shall be duly paid you. In the meantime, my Lieutenant General shall be in my stead, than whom never prince commanded a more noble or worthy subject; not doubting but by your obedience to my General, by your concord in the camp and your valour in the field, we shall shortly have a famous victory over those enemies of my God, of my kingdom and of my people.'

A rousing cheer prevented her from adding anything further, which was perhaps as well, given the tears that were welling in her throat. Robert assisted her back to ground level, kissed her hand, then escorted her back to her horse before helping her back onto it and leading it, still on foot, back out through the fort entrance. The cheers were still echoing as they allowed the royal escort to catch up with them and Elizabeth looked down at Robert.

'How went that, say you?' she asked.

Robert smiled as an attendant handed him the reins of his own horse. 'You were right about one thing, my Lady. You should have married me when you had the opportunity. As for the rest, time will tell, but if any of those men back there die defending England, they will have done so with the blessing of its finest ever monarch ringing in their ears.'

XXI

Elizabeth sat back limply in the specially padded chair in her Bedchamber, the letter slipping from her grasp and sliding onto knees covered by her nightdress, as tears misted her vision yet again. She could not have recounted how many times she had read it and could, if called upon, have recited it word for word. It had been sent by Robert from what he had intended to be his overnight chamber at Cornbury Park, nestled near Oxford, deep in the Cotswold Hills and had been written only the day after he had taken his leave of her in order to take the healing waters at a spa in Derbyshire. It eerily foreshadowed what was to happen that night.

'My sweet,' it read, 'I must once again beg your forgiveness for a deception. For some time now I have been much troubled by a weakness of the stomach, which at times yields me such pain that I am wont to double over and cry out. It would have served neither us, nor England, were I to have disclosed either its existence, or its true nature, to you, but my physician believes it to be a canker and has advised that I take the waters at Buxton, hence my hasty departure.

'Nothing but that could have kept me from your side during these triumphant weeks in which the nation glories in your defiance of the Spanish Philip. You are rightly lauded as 'Gloriana' and our new breed of playwrights are falling over each other to depict your — and England's — greatness. But to me you will always remain my "Lillibet" and as my days draw hastily to a close I am buoyed up in my dreams by memories of those long hot summer days in the copse at Hatfield and later in your chambers in Whitehall. I fear that we shall never again meet in this life, but be assured that I shall await you in the next, when you may cast aside your duties to your adoring people and be with me at long last and for all time.

'Should you remember me with fondness, please be gracious to my son in all but blood, the Courtly and dashing Robert Devereux. He is the apple of his mother's eye and the hope of all my ambition and he wears his Earldom with all the grace that God has seen fit to bestow upon him.

'As the candle in my chamber grows dim, so I feel the candle of my life guttering to an end and I therefore take my earthly leave of you knowing that had the affairs of State not prevented it, we would have been the happiest couple in the whole of the realm.

'As ever, your loving Robin,

'Robert Dudley, by Elizabeth's good grace, Earl of Leicester.'

And now Robert was dead; the doleful messenger had arrived only that morning, carrying the vellum along with the dire tidings that could scarcely be believed. That she dared not believe. That she would not believe.

If it was true, then recent events counted for nothing. The Armada had been scattered by the wind all the way around the English and Irish coasts and very few of the awesome flotilla of ships that had set out from Corunna had succeeded in limping back there. Spain was no longer an immediate threat and England's reputation was restored in Holland, where renewed efforts to overthrow the Spanish yoke had been inspired by England's example. Elizabeth was now the most revered woman in England and scarcely a theatre anywhere in the nation was now staging a new production that did not have as its muse the almost mythical 'Fairy Queen' who never aged, or the 'Virgin Queen' who smote her enemies dead with her sword of righteousness and justice.

But Robert was dead and it all tasted like sawdust. Dear, sweet Robin, who she had treated so badly while loving him so dearly. Had he really understood that it was in England's best interests that she marry royally and had he been able to appreciate that her failure to marry anyone was because anyone other than Robert would have been a pale substitute? She could understand his need to marry only too well, since her own carnal urges had been her private cross for many a year, but had now mercifully receded into memory as her body aged like a wilting daffodil left too long in a vase. She must bring Lettice, Countess of Leicester, back to Court and she would certainly show favour to her young son Essex, because Robert had asked her to. He would serve as Robert's enduring memory, since Robert himself was dead.

Dead. Lost to her sight. Beyond where she could not even tremble when he kissed her hand like a loyal subject, but with the burning desire of the man who had once known her body, after a fashion. If he would only appear through that door, he could have all of her now and she would have their union proclaimed from every church steeple, every rooftop, every castle battlement. But Robert was dead.

The fatal, dread, unwilled, word repeated through her head like a funeral toll, as she slid between the bed sheets and gave vent to the silent tears of loss and regret.

'You must do something, cousin!' Blanche Parry urged Cecil with flapping hands and swirling sleeves as she confronted him in his ground floor chambers. 'She's been in there for three days now and refuses all blandishments to hold audience, eat, or even rise from her bed. It's like she's lost to the nation and willing her own death. You're the man who can most influence her. She heeds your advice, always. For God's mercy, William, do something!'

The young clerks in the outer chamber bowed their heads to hide their amusement at the entertaining scene, almost like a Courtly comedy. Their master Cecil was now bent with age, the sparse white hair that strayed from under his bonnet betraying his almost seventy years, while his cousin Blanche Parry was almost ten years his senior, a clucking old biddy who children might fear as a witch. They were engaged in an argumentative confrontation worthy of an old married couple in dispute about what to have for supper, although the cause of their disagreement was of crucial import for the nation. The Queen had locked her Withdrawing Chamber door and was refusing to come out.

'Can you not enter by way of the kitchen stairs?' Cecil protested.

Blanche would have jumped up in the air in her frustration, had her spindly legs been fit for the task. 'She has barred that also. You must talk her out, William — she will heed your counsel, surely?'

An hour later, Elizabeth had remained silent in response to every blandishment that Cecil yelled through the locked door, to the considerable amusement of the pages in attendance in the Audience Chamber. Eventually, angry, frustrated and belittled, Cecil turned angrily to the page closest to him and yelled an instruction: 'Ask the Captain of the Palace Guard to attend upon us.'

When the formidable looking warrior appeared at his side, Cecil gestured towards the door. 'Can it be broken down, say you?'

The man blanched as he nodded. 'Of course, but Her Majesty...'

'I will bear the consequences,' Cecil told him. 'Have it broken down immediately, then send a carpenter to repair the damage.'

Three heavy blows with a massive broadsword put paid to the old lock and as Cecil raised a shaky leg to kick it open, the door swung inwards to reveal Elizabeth, a heavy cloak over her night attire, standing on the other side with a grim face.

'In my younger days that would have been accounted treason, Cecil. Have a care that you do not forfeit your head in your declining years.'

'Dear Lady,' Cecil replied, 'take my head as a gift, if it will persuade you to return to Council. There is much to discuss, most notably regarding affairs in Ireland and we need your guidance.'

'What you mean is that Council needs my approval for whatever it wishes to do. Let us not pretend that it is my wisdom that you seek. Were I wise, I would now have an heir of my own body to inherit my throne.'

'And that is another matter which must be debated,' Cecil reminded her. 'It is, after all, your Council and it can discuss nothing without your presence.'

'Nonsense, Cecil,' Elizabeth replied. 'You forget that it has met several times in the past when I have been indisposed. And the soreness within my bones today suggests that this must happen again in the future, if God will not, in His infinite mercy, take me before then.'

'My Lady,' Blanche urged her, 'you must eat and then we must prepare you to show yourself again.'

Elizabeth sniggered ironically. 'Indeed we must, for they would shrink back in horror were they to see me like this. What hour is it?'

'It wants of ten of the clock, Your Majesty,' Cecil told her, greatly relieved by the course that events were taking. 'If I might suggest that I convene Council for immediately after dinner?'

'Yes,' Elizabeth conceded wearily, 'do that and see that my Council are served their dinner in the Council Chamber. As for me, Blanche, perhaps a few curds. Or even fish. Certainly nothing that I might be required to chew, since both my stomach and my teeth rebel at the prospect. And now, if you would excuse me, Master Secretary, I must make an effort to once again play the part of "Gloriana" for the benefit of my people.'

Three hours later, Elizabeth stared blankly down the table, hearing the murmur of voices raised to give her worldly advice while her active brain was focused on the seat that would once have been occupied by a loyal and ever-loving Robert. In the seat he previously occupied was Robert Cecil, her 'Pygmy', who would before much longer no doubt expect to inherit his father's office. Walsingham was there as usual, looking more dead than alive and her Lord Chancellor, Sir Christopher Hatton, who had played such an important role in securing the conviction for treason of Mary of Scotland. Elizabeth smiled to herself at the thought that Mary would always be remembered for her beauty in her mature years — preserved for all time as the gracious lady that she was when her head was removed. Not like Elizabeth, who was being forced to stumble into old age like the rest of the fossils ranged down her Council table, betrayed by Father Time into revealing the ugliness for which she would be remembered.

'The ragged beggars, Your Majesty?' Cecil prompted her and Elizabeth came back to the business in hand when she realised that all eyes were on her. 'What of them?' she asked.

Lord Chancellor Hatton realised that he would need to repeat himself. 'They are roaming the nation, Your Majesty, begging for the most part, but — or so it is feared — they will soon become footpads and a cause for fear among honest men.'

'Who are they and how come they to be begging?' Elizabeth asked, to an embarrassed silence. 'Well?' she demanded of Hatton, who bowed his head slightly in reply.

'They once served in your Navy, Your Majesty. The same Navy that defeated the Armada. Many of them lost limbs in the process and are now unable to work for their livelihood. Most of them also have wives and families and all are close to starvation. It is proposed that we allocate money for a relief fund of some sort, from which they might claim a few pennies weekly for bread.'

'And have we the money?' Elizabeth demanded, at which Hatton lowered his eyes to the table. 'Clearly, we do not,' Elizabeth confirmed, 'so how can it be argued that we give what we do not have to those who have even less? And if I hear the word "taxation" I shall be sorely displeased.'

In the awkward silence that followed, Elizabeth raised her chin in challenge. 'This is England, is it not? The proud nation that sent Philip of Spain packing? A nation of warriors worthy of the mantle of ancient Sparta. They found the courage to face Spain — now they must employ it further to fend off starvation. What next falls for our consideration?'

'Ireland, Your Majesty,' Walsingham chimed in. 'Following the unsuccessful Munster Rebellion by the Earl of Desmond, some thirty thousand Irishmen and their families have died of starvation.'

Elizabeth snorted. 'Given that we have just agreed that we cannot grant arms to our own starving, you are not seriously about to suggest that we feed the fallen of that rude and barbarous pack of Catholic dogs?'

'Indeed not, Your Majesty,' Walsingham hastened to explain. 'It is merely that their perilous plight has made them even more rebellious. We burn their crops, scorch their earth and hang their leaders, but they spring up again like weeds in a water meadow. They gave sanctuary to a few Spanish vessels that made it around the north coast of Scotland last year and they remain forever a possible land base should Philip renew his attack upon us.'

'Then we must scorch and starve them even more energetically, must we not?' Elizabeth demanded. 'Who commands our forces in Ireland?'

'The Earl of Sussex was our last commander in the field,' Robert Cecil reminded her, 'until we unwisely allowed the Earl of Tyrone to govern his own people in your name. The Irish, it seems, will always fight among themselves and this latest rebellion arose from nothing more than a family dispute. It was not good counsel.'

'It was the counsel of the late Earl of Leicester,' Elizabeth announced coldly down the table, as Cecil shook his head sadly at his son's folly. 'He was among our finest soldiers and if you would care to undertake the mission, you would be most welcome to take yourself off to Ireland and clean up this latest mess.'

Robert Cecil shook his head. 'I am no soldier, Your Majesty,' he admitted.

'Indeed you are not, Pygmy, so perhaps it was not wise of you to doubt the wisdom of one who was. You may all leave the choice of a suitable Governor General for Ireland to me. Now, since I grow fatigued, what is next on the list, Cecil?'

'Finally, the matter of the inheritance, Your Majesty,' Cecil replied, to faintly audible groans around the table. The Queen was displaying petulance enough, without the need for this touchy matter to be raised again.

Elizabeth glared down the table. 'So how go our negotiations with Scotland, Walsingham?' she demanded.

Walsingham cleared his throat of the phlegm that seemed to accumulate in it freely these days and advised Council in a reedy voice of the outcome of his latest diplomatic foray to Linlithgow. 'Middling well, so far as can be measured. King James seems to have accepted the death of his mother, who of course he hardly knew, but he is inclined to regard the offer of the English throne as some sort of recompense, or expiation of sin. Were he Catholic, he would no doubt see it as a penance.'

'But he is not, else he would not be my chosen successor,' Elizabeth retorted hotly. 'I am merely following the dearest wish of my late father, that Tudors should rule England in perpetuity. Since his mother was the granddaughter of my Aunt Margaret, he has the most Tudor blood flowing through his veins. You say that he accepts, Walsingham? Does he also accept that he will not climb onto the English throne until I die naturally, or by whatever means God shall determine, or think you that he is minded to bring forward the date of his accession by invasion?'

'He will wait, Majesty, and he assures me of his discretion.'

'Good. Then, since I was advised that this was the only remaining item of business, we are done, I think. We meet again a week today; see to it, Cecil,' she added as she rose from her chair and everyone in Council rose and bowed.

'Sir Walter has been waiting several days for an audience', Blanche Parry told Elizabeth as she was about to pass swiftly through the Audience Chamber to her Withdrawing Chamber. Blanche was hopeful that by diverting her attention she might prevent her mistress from once again taking to her bed, and she was also embarrassed by the number of excuses she had been obliged to make to explain her absence. As a gentle reminder to Elizabeth that her time was not her own, Blanche gestured with a slight jerk of the head towards the Courtly gentleman sitting by the fire with a mug of mulled wine and chewing half-heartedly on a wafer.

The long-patient, and ever courteous, Sir Walter Raleigh was a favourite of Elizabeth's, not least because he only ever seemed to bring her glad tidings. He had served her well as one of her major landholders in Ireland, one of the English nobles granted vast tracts of largely unworkable bog in return for their efforts in suppressing the ever rebellious natives. He had been knighted partly for this, but most notably for his enthusiasm to open up the east coast of the Americas to English colonists. Although something of a dreamer, he knew how to dream in a manner that pleased his vain Queen and his proposal that any newly settled land be named 'Virginia' had sat well in her ears.

'How go things across the ocean, Sir Walter?' Elizabeth asked politely as she walked towards him.

He rose, bowed and kissed the offered hand. 'I have much to report, Your Majesty, but chief among them is that I have recently learned of a land in the south of the American vastness that contains a city constructed entirely of gold. I am here today to request the grant of a monopoly to seek it out, exploit it and share the riches with England.'

'Consider it granted, Sir Walter,' Elizabeth beamed back gratefully, 'and I will not deny that at this time England could well do with such an increase in wealth. Seek out my Chancellor Sir Christopher Hatton and have him draft the necessary document. Also, please accept my sincere apology for the length of time you have been kept waiting, but there were urgent matters of State that required my attention.'

The audience continued in this polite vein for a few more minutes and was then terminated due to the desire of each of them to be elsewhere. Raleigh in order to secure the drafting of his monopoly and Elizabeth to retreat once more to her bed.

The Banquet and Ball to celebrate Elizabeth's thirty years on the throne, even though it had taken so long to organise that it was now almost thirty-one years, was drawing to a sated, limp and sweaty close and Elizabeth could, without too much further provocation, have screamed her boredom out loud. The musicians were so exhausted that they were not always quite in time with each other, the feet of the dancers had begun to drag and the Fool had run through his repertoire at least three times without making her laugh once. She had toothache, a headache and a churning in her bowels that would soon demand a closed stool. And that idiot Essex was still prancing around like a rabbit caught on hot coals, praising her beauty to the skies and seeking to prove to all around them that he was her clear favourite. The pathetic old woman drawn to young flesh with shapely calves and a subtly stuffed codpiece. A dandy who was all mouth and no cock of his own.

She tolerated him because something about him reminded her of Robert. He was not of Robert's flesh, but he had learned to mimic some of his carefree manner and on a good day he somehow contrived to bring alive the dear memory of the father substitute who had been twice the real man he would ever be. Robert Devereux, Earl of Essex, fop, braggart and painful reminder that her world was sliding into shit by the day.

She was aware of all the nudges, winks, giggles and whispered indelicacies. Of the rumours that circulated among the kitchens, outhouses and stables that Essex crept into her Bedchamber every night to replace his mother's husband between the royal thighs. It would have been amusing, had it not been so laughable. Be that as it may, she found such ribald fantasies easier to bear than the false fawning that Essex seemed to have encouraged in all the other male Courtiers, as they pretended to be dazzled by her beauty, which had allegedly only grown with the years rather than diminished. Either they were seeking advancement by way of flattery, or they had fallen prey to a collective sickness that deprived men of their eyesight.

She was sorely tempted to challenge the worst of them to attend in her Withdrawing Chamber while Blanche and her other Ladies were preparing her for bed. Off would come the layers of rich outer clothing, the pendants, chains, rings and brooches, all to be safely stored away overnight. Then the under garments that were usually stained dark with the sweat of that certain age in a woman's life when the flushes came and went like Spring tides. There was still a tall body underneath, but it was now stately rather than lithe, lumpy rather than virgin smooth. How could one retain one's virginity while losing the smoothness that allegedly came with it?

Then down to the ultimate horror that would make any man's cock grow limp at the prospect that lay before him. The flowing red hair would be lifted off and placed reverently on a wooden effigy of her head, to retain its shape for the following morning when it would again be lowered onto the scratchy grey patches that remained of her own hair, long lost to the smallpox. Finally the ceruse would be scraped off her face to reveal the pockmarks from that same pestilence, as the girls performing the task tried to ensure that they remained upwind of her poisonous breath. Altogether a far from tempting prospect for a young buck accustomed to the chubby thighs, rounded titties and false encouragements of alehouse whores.

The idiot was back by her side, kissing her hand, pawing her arm and seeking to push it back to the point at which the back of his hand could brush against her breast. She pushed back firmly but there was no stopping him.

'Would that Your Gracious Majesty would grant me some way in which I could demonstrate my undying love of your ever beautiful and entrancing person.' Elizabeth choked back the laughter with what hopefully sounded like a grunt of pleasure.

'What had you in mind, my Lord?' she asked. Something fatal, I hope, said her brain.

'Perhaps to lead your valiant army into yet further glorious conquest somewhere abroad?' he asked hopefully, provoking a wicked idea in her mind.

'Your stepfather proved his valour in Ireland,' she reminded him. 'It has grown fractious again since his death. Perhaps you would consent to follow in his illustrious footsteps?'

'Gladly — freely — willingly!' Essex enthused and Elizabeth took his hand in hers, pressed it against her full breasts and summoned up a husky whisper.

'Then, if you come back triumphant, we may see where else your success might lead.'

He bowed graciously and slipped from the presence, eager to tell his hangers-on about his latest favour from their Queen. Wondering if she had misread the fear in his eyes, Elizabeth turned to Blanche Parry, then nudged her awake where she was dozing with her elbow on the side table.

'Time to bring this misery to an end, my dear friend,' she muttered as they both rose and made their way through the wilting throng of exhausted Courtiers who were smiling at the prospect that they too might now leave without offending their Queen.

I'm sorry, Robert, she apologised in her head as she passed through the double doors towards the stairs that led to her chambers, but you raised such a tiresome and brainless fool who is not worthy of even your memory.

XXII

Elizabeth picked listlessly at the slice of cinnamon manchet loaf and selected a plum while staring at the latest portrait of her on the far wall of her Withdrawing Chamber and wondering who it was meant to represent. Another false image of someone who didn't exist. It had not captured the essential young girl underneath all the finery, because she had ceased to be visible years ago. Nor was it honest enough to reproduce the hideous hag that time had turned her into, because the artist, like most of the others who had preceded him, was either seeking to ingratiate himself with her, or was terrified of the Tower if he painted what he saw.

This combination of hope of advancement or fear of disfavour was now holding the nation together as she sought to rule alone, in the absence of all those who had died and left her to manage its affairs without their comfort, support and wise counsel. First to go had been darling Robert, then Cecil, followed by Walsingham a year later. In between the two, God had finally relieved dear Blanche Parry of her aches and pains and there was no-one among her current Ladies in whom Elizabeth felt confident to confide. Likewise there was no-one in her Council whom she did not suspect of self-interest in the advice they gave her, most of it bad.

Thanks to their urgings, Drake had been sent — against his own advice — to hit back at Spain with an Armada of England's own and had lost half his men and a third of his ships in a catastrophic defeat that had only served to encourage Philip to rebuild with a view to launching another attack that was expected at any time. There was no money for England to do likewise, given a run of poor harvests and increasing resistance to new taxes. The Catholics refused to sit quietly under a Protestant regime and most of the daily reports brought to her by the ailing Chancellor Hatton were of covert Jesuit priests being dragged from their hiding places in manor houses throughout the realm and summarily done to death on the lawns in front of the families who had been hiding them. If her people still truly loved her, it was only out of fear of the consequences if they did not and what sort of love was that?

Life went on as if this was still the 'Golden Age' that the nation's poets and playwrights were celebrating, but the reality was that government of the realm had been reduced to competition for patronage and preference, and the granting of monopolies to already wealthy nobles that drove up the prices for everything and led to resentment among the common people. The fact that they hadn't yet risen up in rebellion reflected only their fear of her and she was ashamed of what her reign had become.

She was unable to dominate her Council because, in the absence of sage men such as Cecil who had her interests at heart, she could not be certain which were the wisest policies and therefore dare not impose her will in favour of one or another. Her weakness in this regard had led to factional strife within what should have been — and once was — a body united for the greater welfare of England.

Most grievous for Elizabeth had been the open warfare between Robert Cecil, the pale imitation of his great father and Robert, Earl of Essex, stepson of the great love of her life. Both had eventually proved false and today she must sign the paper that lay at her elbow — the paper that would send the dynastic hope of dear Robert to his death for treason.

214

Robert Devereux had lost little time in proving that he was no soldier, as he blustered and blundered his way through a series of uprisings in Ireland with an arrogant rule of fist that made him as much reviled by his own men as he was hated by the enemy Irish. Despite her stern order that he remain at his post, he had deserted his command and returned to the softer pastures of London, where he presented himself with a flourish, as if expecting to be welcomed home as a hero. Instead, he was treated to the same humiliation that his stepfather had endured in the Low Countries, when he was obliged to stand, head bowed, while his uncle William Knollys, Earl of Banbury and a fellow Council member, read out a report that condemned him for desertion of duty and consigned him to house arrest in his own York House in London.

Elizabeth added to the humiliation by stripping him of the monopolies he had wheedled out of her in her weaker moments when she was reminded of his beloved stepfather who still visited her in her dreams. All this had at least put paid to further rumours that they shared a bed, but Robert had reacted with the petulant bitterness that ruled his life and had conducted a secret conspiracy with certain Catholic malcontents in London to seize the Queen's person and invite King James of Scotland to assume the throne of England earlier that anticipated. Robert Cecil's spies kept watch on him and it was a gloating Robert Cecil who insisted on Essex's trial for treason and thereafter kept up an irresistible barrage of demands for his execution that threatened to disrupt all other Council business until Elizabeth relented.

She took the warrant in her left hand, picked up her quill, dipped it into the inkstand and signed it. Then the thought crossed her mind that had she married Robert Dudley, any son of theirs could have turned out like Essex. She had just consigned to the block the closest thing she still had to the man who had loved her most truly and she spat the small mouthful of manchet loaf onto the damask cloth before it could choke her.

Elizabeth transferred herself, at her own stubborn request, to Richmond Palace, there to mourn the latest death in a gloomy seclusion that not even her closest Ladies could persuade her to abandon. She had received news of the untimely demise of her long serving Lady, Catherine Howard, Countess of Nottingham. As Catherine Carey she had been the granddaughter of Mary Boleyn and according to rumour the illegitimate descendant of Elizabeth's own father Henry VIII. On either account they had been cousins and Catherine had served Elizabeth as First Lady of the Bedchamber for over thirty years. She had also been the wife of Elizabeth's trusted Admiral of the Fleet, Lord Howard of Effingham, during the glorious defeat of the Armada, and somehow her death symbolised the decline of the Golden Age and the decay of all the fond memories to which Elizabeth had been clinging in her increasing battles with melancholia.

A melancholia that had seemed to begin with the revelation that Robert Dudley had left an illegitimate son — the direct fruit of his loins and the product of his affair with Baroness Sheffield. His name was also Robert and he had been hidden away abroad until his mother had launched a lawsuit in which she claimed to have been married to his father and was supporting the young Robert's claims to his father's estates of Kenilworth and Warwick. Elizabeth had been stricken to the core by the realisation that another woman had born Robert's child and seen him grow into manhood. She could have had all that for herself, had not some ill wind blown her the crown of England.

The death of Catherine Howard somehow plunged the knife in deeper, reviving stories of the sexual freedom that her father Henry had enjoyed and which had been denied to her. Her Ladies began to experience difficulty in persuading her to eat and dish after dish was sent back down to the kitchens untouched. The Cook had to be personally reassured by the new Senior Lady, the Marchioness of Northampton, that this was not due to any fear on the part of Her Majesty that she might be poisoned.

There was soon much more that Elizabeth's Ladies had to explain to a curious staff at Richmond, in the hope that the truth would not rock the realm, or provoke some sort of uprising. The stark reality was that Her Majesty was no longer in quite her right mind.

It had begun ominously enough with Elizabeth insisting on standing for hours on end in her Bedchamber, mumbling to herself and refusing all offers of food and drink, as if determined to starve herself to death. She insisted, however, on being fully dressed, bewigged and cerused, and swore in language more suited to the alehouse on the several occasions when it was politely suggested that she should allow her surgeon to examine her. She would stand in this manner for many hours, until her legs gave way under her and her closest attendants took to placing cushions on the floor in anticipation.

She was only visited once by Robert Cecil, to whom she replied only in monosyllables when he sought her approval for various matters. Sensing that all was not well, he politely suggested that she might consider taking to her bed, to which she replied defiantly that she did not intend to do so. When he pressed his point with 'But Your Majesty must, for the sake of her health,' she screamed back at him 'Must is not a word to use to princes, little man' and he hastily withdrew from the presence with a sad shake of the head towards Lady Northampton on his way out.

Things deteriorated further when Elizabeth began hallucinating. One morning Lady Northampton bowed into the presence to find Elizabeth already seated on the pile of cushions and staring at the far wall. 'I don't suppose you can see what I see, Helena, but my father and sister have come on a visit. It is for me alone to witness, since they have high matters of State to reveal. My father smiles and says that I am his true daughter, while my sister Mary, as usual, chides me for my religion.'

Lady Northampton wasn't sure whether to go along with this, or to try to talk some sense into her mistress, but before she could decide there was more.

'Here comes the Scots Mary, smiling in triumph because her son will bid for my crown. We never met and I wish you could see her, for I would wish to know if she was so beautiful as she is to me today. I regret me that I had her put to death and I curse the day that I signed that warrant.'

Elizabeth's bewildered and embarrassed Ladies could only wait and see how events would turn out, since every effort they made to bring their mistress back to reality was met with wild curses, not always decently worded. But then came the day when their opportunity presented itself.

'I may finally take to my bed,' Elizabeth announced, 'since Robert is here with me and he tells me that my time is come.'

They needed no further encouragement and the clothes were hastily stripped from her where she stood, including the heavily soiled undergarments. She smelled even worse than usual, given her lifelong suspicion of bathing even in good times, but they persevered and eventually got her between the sheets in her nightgown, still wearing her wig and refusing all offers to remove the ceruse from her bony face. Only Lady Northampton remained and Elizabeth beckoned her to the side of the bed, before instructing her in a firm voice that belied the state of her mind.

'There must be no physicians when I die.'

'My Lady?'

'No man shall be permitted to examine between my legs after I am dead, since none did during my lifetime.'

Helena tried not to chuckle, in case it wasn't intended as a jest, and would only later conjecture in her own mind whether Elizabeth was anxious for no-one to learn that she had been living a lie as the 'Virgin Queen' and wished to take that secret to her grave.

Over the next few days, Elizabeth seemed to sink into a morbid torpor, refusing to eat with angry shakes of the head whenever sustenance was offered to her. It was obvious that the end was near and Archbishop Whitgift was called in to say prayers with her while musicians played softly at the back of the Bedchamber. Word was sent to Council and Robert Cecil was ushered into the sick room while the Queen appeared to be still alive and he asked her about her succession. Receiving no verbal response, he prompted, 'James of Scotland?' and Elizabeth raised a shaky hand and drew the symbol of a crown round her head. Then she appeared to fall into a deep sleep from which she never awoke and the only indication of the moment of death came with a long sigh of apparent relief.

Uneasily aware that her late mistress might have wished to take certain secrets to her grave, Lady Northampton insisted on sorting through the personal and intimate items left in the

219

various receptacles in her bedchamber. In a drawer to the side of Elizabeth's former bed she discovered the heavily creased vellum on which Robert Dudley had composed his communication to her from Cornbury Park during his last evening of life. She had kept it closely concealed and had written on the top of it, in her own florid hand, 'His last letter.'

The proclamation of the Queen's passing was read out loud by Robert Cecil, first at Whitehall, then at St Paul's, then finally in Cheapside. Given that she had been seventy years old at her passing, there were few among the people of London who had known any other monarch and they packed the streets to demonstrate their grief at the passing of 'Gloriana'. Her body having been embalmed, it was transported upriver to Whitehall in a lead coffin to await burial, while detailed arrangements were made for an elaborate funeral for an outgoing monarch and a rich reception for the incoming James of Scotland, who lost no time in heading south to claim his inheritance.

The short funeral procession from Westminster Palace to Westminster Abbey had echoes of Elizabeth's coronation procession all those years ago, although of course the identities of the one thousand official mourners were different from those who had cheered her onto the throne. And again no expense was spared, as a coffin draped in the richest purple velvet was carried on a hearse drawn by four horses decked out in black velvet. Lying on the top of the coffin was an effigy of Elizabeth herself and the crowds gasped as it passed slowly by them carrying a visual representation of a Queen they had all loved, but few of them had ever glimpsed.

Elizabeth was to be interred alongside the body of her long dead sister Mary, the woman whose persecution of her had converted a simple light-hearted girl into a suspicious and at times paranoid shrew of a woman who had opted for celibacy after witnessing what marriage had done to her sister. The inscription on their joint epitaph read 'Consorts in realm and tomb, here we sleep, Elizabeth and Mary, sisters, in hope of resurrection.'

A NOTE TO THE READER

Dear Reader,

Thank you for reading this final novel in my Tudor series, and I hope it lived up to your expectations. Elizabeth Tudor was a complex character, but history has assigned her a one-sided epitaph, assisted by talented actresses such as Glenda Jackson, Cate Blanchet and Judi Dench, who have given us such a memorable visual image of a strong woman dominating a male world. Hopefully this novel has redressed the balance somewhat.

A different Elizabeth began to emerge as I was researching for this novel. I did what I normally do, which is to examine the established facts and then imagine the effect that those events would have had on the character whose actions they dictated. For Elizabeth, the situation in which she found herself in 1558 would have been challenging, and seemingly beyond her ability to surmount.

Although the death of her half-sister Queen Mary was not entirely unexpected, England looked to Elizabeth to take the reins of power without breaking stride, and she was ill-equipped to rise to the occasion. Barely twenty-five years of age, she had been held in the background by a highly suspicious Mary. Elizabeth therefore came to the throne with little experience of life at Court, no exposure to the major issues that confronted her nation, and very few genuine allies she could trust, and upon whom she might rely. And she had to come to terms very quickly with three major concerns.

The first was the corrosive religious divide that had marked the reigns of her three immediate predecessors. England had been divorced from Catholic Rome by her father Henry, and the new Protestant faith had been thrust down the peoples' throats by her half-brother Edward. Mary had sought to guide the nation back under the wing of the Pope, and had dealt harshly with those who sought to oppose her. The nation was now anxiously waiting to see what policy Elizabeth would adopt, but her personal wish was to allow her subjects to worship according to their individual consciences. As she was shortly to discover, the diehard Catholics lying in wait for her — most particularly those in Scotland and France — would not allow her this luxury, and forced her hand into actions that she found both stressful and unpalatable.

Associated with this issue was the broader one of England's relations with more powerful nations across the Channel. France would harbour Mary Stuart and her Catholic ambition to rule England, while Spain would prove less than friendly. King Philip of Spain had, until Mary's death, been the consort joint monarch of England, and he would not easily relinquish his ambition to add England to the Habsburg portfolio of nations. Elizabeth lost little time in rejecting his marriage proposal, thereby exposing England to the risk of invasion that would eventuate in the later years of her reign. But the availability of the hand of the 'Virgin Queen' was the third major issue with which the beautiful young heiress had to contend.

The entire Tudor era was dominated by the need to produce heirs, and Elizabeth's period as the final Tudor monarch was no different. She was constantly harassed by her Council of State with polite requests that she take a husband, and preferably a suitable one from a European royal house. But very few eligible ones existed, and the ones who did were not to her taste. On top of all her other challenges, Elizabeth had to come to terms with the fact that the man she really yearned for — Robert Dudley — was first of all already married, and then rendered available by the death of his first wife in circumstances that made it diplomatically impossible for them to wed.

If ever a nervous young woman thrust into the most senior role in the nation required those around her that she could trust implicitly, it was Elizabeth. And God at least smiled upon her in that regard. England under Elizabeth would have presented future historians with a totally different picture had it not been for William Cecil, Elizabeth's Chief Minister, guide, mentor and friend. Not only was he a very able administrator presiding over an efficient public service, but he was totally loyal. However, even he was insistent that Elizabeth marry, and her instinct and experience thus far inclined her to Robert Dudley, who in Courtly terms was forbidden fruit. We can only imagine what she suffered in her determination to keep him at arms' length for the sake of her public image, and it is more than likely that she found comfort in the unswerving and unassuming natural friendship of her Chief Lady, Blanche Parry.

So behind the 'Gloriana' facade we see a different kind of Elizabeth. A young woman cursed by her natural beauty and earlier life into being considered frivolous and sensual, who was forced by circumstances to override popular perception and rule with a rod of steel, armed with the loyal and constant guidance of the only three people she could trust. I hope that my 'take' on Elizabeth did not shatter too many of your preconceptions.

As ever, I look forward to receiving feedback from you, whether in the form of a review on **Amazon** or **Goodreads**. Or, of course, you can try the more personal approach on my website, and my Facebook page: **DavidFieldAuthor**.

Happy reading!

David

davidfieldauthor.com

Sapere Books is an exciting new publisher of brilliant fiction and popular history.

To find out more about our latest releases and our monthly bargain books visit our website: **saperebooks.com**

Manufactured by Amazon.ca
Bolton, ON